THE RAIN DRAGON RESCUE

THE IMAGINARY VETERINARY: BOOK 3

BY SUZANNE SELFORS

ILLUSTRATIONS BY DAN SANTAT

Little, Brown and Company
New York Boston

ALSO BY SUZANNE SELFORS:

The Imaginary Veterinary Series
The Sasquatch Escape
The Lonely Lake Monster
The Rain Dragon Rescue
The Order of the Unicorn

The Smells Like Dog Series
Smells Like Dog
Smells Like Treasure
Smells Like Pirates

To Catch a Mermaid
Fortune's Magic Farm

Text copyright © 2014 by Suzanne Selfors
Illustrations copyright © 2014 by Dan Santat
Text in excerpt from *The Order of the Unicorn* copyright © 2014 by Suzanne Selfors
Illustrations in excerpt from *The Order of the Unicorn* copyright © 2014 by Dan Santat

Little, Brown and Company

Hachette Book Group
237 Park Avenue, New York, NY 10017
Visit our website at lb-kids.com

Little, Brown and Company is a division of Hachette Book Group, Inc.
The Little, Brown name and logo are trademarks of Hachette Book Group, Inc.

The publisher is not responsible for websites
(or their content) that are not owned by the publisher.

First Paperback Edition: June 2014
First published in hardcover in January 2014 by Little, Brown and Company

Library of Congress Cataloging-in-Publication Data

Selfors, Suzanne.
  The rain dragon rescue / by Suzanne Selfors ; illustrations by Dan Santat.—First edition.
    pages cm.—(The imaginary veterinary ; book 3)
  Summary: "Ten-year-olds Ben and Pearl continue their apprenticeships at Dr. Woo's Worm Hospital, where they meet a dragon named Metalmouth and get a chance to travel to the Imaginary World"—Provided by publisher.
  ISBN 978-0-316-22557-1 (hc)—ISBN 978-0-316-22555-7 (e-book) —ISBN 978-0-316-22549-6 (pb)
  [1. Dragons—Fiction. 2. Imaginary creatures—Fiction. 3. Veterinarians—Fiction. 4. Apprentices—Fiction.] I. Santat, Dan, illustrator. II. Title.
  PZ7.S456922Rai 2014
  [Fic]—dc23

                                                                      2013012134

10 9 8 7 6 5 4 3 2 1

RRD-C

Printed in the United States of America

For rain dragons everywhere

CONTENTS

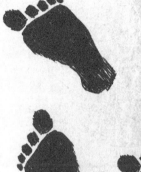

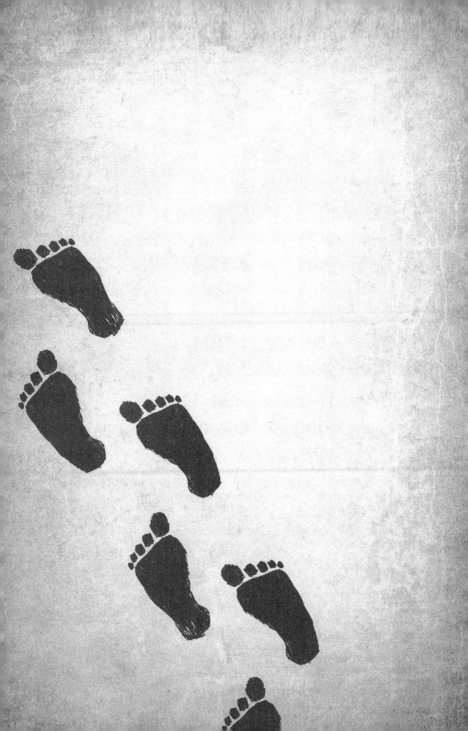

1

It sounded like claws scratching against the side of the house.

Giant claws.

Ben's eyes flew open. *Where am I?* he wondered. The room was inky black, thanks to a pair of heavy curtains that blocked the moonlight. The mattress felt lumpy, and the quilt smelled like mothballs. Only one thing was recognizable—the soft gnawing sound of Snooze, Ben's hamster, as he chewed a toilet paper tube. It wasn't unusual for Snooze to be wide awake in the middle of the night. He was nocturnal, after all. But the other noise?

Screeeeeeech.

Had a window just opened?

Ben sat up and clutched the pillow to his chest. As his eyes adjusted, he remembered that this wasn't his regular bedroom. No glow-in-the-dark stars on the ceiling, no dinosaur-shaped nightlight in the corner, no mother or father down the hall to ask, "What's going on out there?" This was the cramped, extra bedroom right next to the kitchen at his grandfather's house.

And the noise had come from...*the kitchen.*

Back in Los Angeles, Ben's father had installed a high-tech home-security system. If anyone tried to break in, alarms would ring and guards would come running. But Grandpa Abe didn't have anything like that. The only alarm system was his black tomcat, Barnaby, who hissed when disturbed.

Hissssssssss.

Uh-oh.

Ben froze. Maybe it would be best to stay in bed. If a burglar had decided to take something from Grandpa Abe's house, then so be it. What could Ben do? He wasn't any good at karate or judo, and he certainly didn't know how to use a lasso. The only time he'd gotten into a fight was when he wrestled Eli Finklebaum to the ground after Eli had cut in front of him, for the umpteenth time, in the snack line at school. It'd been bad enough having to wait ten minutes to get a bag of chips, but to have Eli snicker and push his way to the front every single day was totally unfair. And when he took the very last bag of Barbecue Curlies, the one Ben had been craving—well, it was an event that the students at Oakview Hebrew Academy still talked about.

Whoooosh.

A sudden burst of orange light glowed beneath the bedroom door, then disappeared. Ben sniffed. Smoke!

He scrambled out of bed. If there was a fire in the kitchen, the door would feel hot. But it was cool to his touch, so very carefully, he cracked it open.

Moonlight trickled in through the front windows. Barnaby stood on the table, surrounded by dirty dishes, his back arched, his fur sticking up as if someone had rubbed a balloon all over it. Tendrils of smoke rose from a singed hole in the tablecloth. Barnaby stared at the counter, hissing like a snake. Ben poked his head out of his bedroom just far enough to get a better view.

At Grandpa Abe's house, the kitchen window was always left halfway open so Barnaby could come and go as he pleased. But on this night it had been opened all the way. And someone was reaching through.

Correction—not someone. Some*thing.*

The intruder's arm was covered in black scales and was long enough to stretch down the counter. Its paw, which was bigger than a Frisbee, had four fingerlike claws.

If it hadn't been for all his adventures over the last few days, Ben might have thought he was going crazy. But he knew, without a doubt, that the creature reaching into his grandfather's house in the middle of the night was a dragon. A real, living, fire-breathing dragon. Ben had seen it before, but never up close. A brave person might have said hello. But Ben would never describe himself as brave. And talking to a dragon in the middle of the night felt risky. "You're a cautious boy," his mother always said. "There's nothing wrong with being cautious."

Ben pressed himself against the wall, his heart flip-flopping as the dragon's claws tapped along the counter. The dragon grabbed a bag of bagels, then tossed it to the floor. It shoved aside a roll of paper towels and a ratty old rag. It moved over plates,

around coffee cups, then paused at the toaster. With a quick yank, it pulled the cord from the wall socket and whisked the toaster right out the window. Outside, a shape moved toward the lawn.

Ben ran to the living room, climbed onto the couch, and peered out the front window. Barnaby stopped hissing and scampered up next to Ben. They both watched as the massive dragon galloped across the grass and took to the sky. Moonlight glinted off the toaster as the creature rose above the rooftops and disappeared from view.

Ben turned and glared at Barnaby. "You saw nothing," he told the cat. "That dragon is our secret."

2

TOASTER TROUBLE

Breakfast with Grandpa Abe is so much better than breakfast back home, Ben thought as he settled into a wobbly kitchen chair. There were no vitamins, no whole-grain muffins, no fresh-squeezed wheatgrass juice. Sugar was the main ingredient. This morning's meal featured a box of rainbow-colored Sugar Loops, a couple of glazed doughnuts, and white bread with strawberry jam. There was just one problem....

"Where's the toaster?" Grandpa Abe asked, pointing at the counter. A rectangle of left-behind crumbs filled the space where the toaster usually sat.

"I don't know," Ben said with a shrug. There was absolutely no way he could tell his grandfather the truth. A real dragon was difficult enough to explain. But why one would want a toaster—well, Ben was still trying to wrap his brain around that question. "Did you put it in a drawer?"

Grandpa Abe rubbed his bald head. "Why would I put my toaster in a drawer?"

"Did you take it to the senior center?" It seemed a reasonable question, since his grandfather spent most days at the Buttonville Senior Center. On Mondays the seniors played bingo, Tuesdays they played board games, and Wednesdays they took dance lessons. On Thursdays they listened to lectures, Fridays were for celebrating birthdays, and Saturdays were dedicated to eating pudding. Ben figured that in between all those activities, they might eat toast.

"I didn't take the toaster anywhere. *Oy vey*, what

a mystery." Grandpa Abe sighed. "I need a lost toaster like I need a hole in my head." He poured coffee into a chipped mug, then joined Ben at the table.

"I'll help you look for it," Ben offered. Before sticking him on the airplane to Buttonville, Ben's parents had given him a small wad of cash, enough for emergencies. He could buy a new toaster at the Buttonville Hardware Store and his grandfather would never know. "I'm good at finding things."

Grandpa Abe's face got all crinkly as he smiled. "Okay by me, but eat your breakfast first."

As his grandfather sipped his coffee, Ben opened the top of Snooze's hamster cage and dropped in a yellow Sugar Loop. He'd set the cage next to his cereal bowl. This would have caused a fuss back home because Ben's mother was convinced that rodents, whether they were of the small hamster variety or the large rat variety, carried ghastly germs. "Wash your hands," she always said after Ben held Snooze. "Don't kiss it or let it get near your food. Those creatures aren't clean." But Grandpa

Abe didn't say a word about germs, and he didn't seem to care if things were clean or not. In fact, the entire kitchen was a mess. The floor was sticky, thanks to spilled coffee and syrup. The stove was covered in splattered grease, and even though Ben had tried to help clean the dishes, the stack in the sink still looked like the Leaning Tower of Pisa. Maybe the mess was why Grandpa Abe hadn't noticed the claw marks on the counter or the singed hole in the tablecloth.

Snooze poked his nose out of his chewed toilet paper tube and grabbed the piece of cereal. Squatting on his round haunches with his nose wiggling, he sank his little teeth into the yellow loop and munched.

"So, boychik," Grandpa Abe said as he added sugar to his coffee. "What are your plans on such a nice day? Are you going to play with Pearl?"

Ben didn't point out that *playing* was something little kids did. He was ten years old, and if he decided to call Pearl, they'd *hang out*. Pearl Petal

was his only friend in the little town of Buttonville. They'd met each other thanks to a great adventure involving an injured dragon hatchling and an escaped sasquatch. Yep. That's right. After coming to Buttonville to stay with his grandfather for the summer, Ben Silverstein discovered that dragon hatchlings and sasquatches really, truly exist. As do leprechauns and lake monsters. And he'd discovered all this thanks to Dr. Emerald Woo, a veterinarian who'd set up her hospital in the old button factory.

The sign on the hospital gate read: DR. WOO'S WORM HOSPITAL. But that was meant to mislead. Dr. Woo didn't take care of worms. She was a veterinarian for Imaginary creatures, and everything that went on inside her hospital was a secret.

Because Ben and Pearl had brilliantly caught the escaped sasquatch, they were offered summer jobs as apprentices. And so, on Mondays, Wednesdays, and Fridays, Ben and Pearl worked from 8 AM to 3 PM, doing all sorts of things that were only supposed to happen in storybooks.

But because they'd each signed a contract of secrecy, they had to zip their lips. That was why Ben couldn't tell his grandfather about last night's intruder.

Today was Tuesday, Ben's day off, so other than buying his grandfather a new toaster and telling Pearl about the dragon sighting, he had no idea what he was going to do. Back home in Los Angeles, he might have invited friends over to swim in his pool. He might have played on his computer or watched television. But since Grandpa Abe didn't have a pool or a computer or a television, Ben was befuddled.

Grandpa Abe cleared his throat. "You gonna sit there all day or are you gonna answer my question? What are your plans?"

Ben fidgeted. If he didn't come up with a plan, his grandfather would make him go to the senior center to play old board games like Scrabble and Monopoly. "Uh, I think I should stay here and take care of Snooze because..." Ben tried to think of a reason. "Because he doesn't want to be left alone.

He had a nightmare last night and he couldn't go back to sleep. I'm guessing he dreamed your cat was trying to eat him."

Right on cue, Barnaby leaped through the kitchen window, then lay on the counter, a small black object clutched in his paws. Normally, Barnaby would bring home a dead rodent of some sort, but this object was flat and shiny. The cat looked right at Ben with a satisfied smile.

He'd found a dragon scale!

"Did you say your mouse had a nightmare?" Grandpa Abe asked, his gray eyebrows rising to the top of his forehead. "How do you know this?"

"He's not a mouse—he's a hamster," Ben corrected, his gaze darting between Grandpa Abe and the cat. "And I can tell it was a nightmare because he was sleep-running. That's like sleep-walking, except faster. This morning he's practically a nervous wreck. He needs me to take care of him."

Snooze didn't look like a nervous wreck. He seemed content chewing his loop.

"Sleep-running?" Grandpa Abe folded his arms and stared over the top of the cereal box. "Benjamin Silverstein, is that one of your stories?"

Ben nodded sheepishly. He'd made up the story because he didn't want to hurt his grandfather's feelings about not wanting to go to the senior center.

Grandpa Abe chuckled. "My grandson, the story-teller." With a groan, he rose from the chair and headed for the coffeemaker. Then he stopped in front of the cat. "What's that thing Barnaby's chewing on?"

But before Ben could come up with another story, a loud voice hollered, "Attention, Buttonville residents! Attention, Buttonville residents! Emergency meeting at Town Hall! Emergency meeting at Town Hall!"

"*Oy gevalt!*" Grandpa Abe exclaimed. "First the toaster, now this. Can't a man drink his coffee in peace?"

3

TURMOIL AT TOWN HALL

mergency meeting!" the voice hollered.

"What do you think's going on?" Ben asked.

"Martha Mulberry is at it again," his grandfather said. "She calls an emergency meeting about once a week."

Ben had met Mrs. Mulberry. She was the town's busiest busybody *and* president of the Welcome Wagon Committee. Though she made it her job to know everything about everyone in Buttonville, she hadn't been able to learn anything about the mysterious Dr. Woo, and Ben intended to keep it that way.

"We'd better go," Grandpa Abe said. "Martha

takes roll call, and if you don't show up, she comes looking for you."

Ben returned Snooze's cage to his bedroom. When he left, he closed the door tight to keep out the cat. Barnaby lay across the counter, gnawing on the dragon scale. Ben, who wanted to avoid a nasty cat bite, didn't try to take the treasure away. "Leave my hamster alone," he whispered in Barnaby's ear. The cat growled softly.

Grandpa Abe put on his moth-eaten cardigan and his canvas hat. After grabbing his cane, he and Ben climbed into the old Cadillac and drove to Main Street.

Town Hall was the tallest building in Buttonville, thanks to its clock tower. Because a pigeon had built its nest on top of the tower, the clock's face was covered in droppings, making it nearly impossible to tell the time. Like most other buildings in Buttonville, Town Hall's paint was faded and chipped, and one of its windows was broken. Stray buttons, leftovers from the factory days, were wedged in the sidewalk cracks out front.

A slow stream of residents climbed the front steps. Ben recognized many of them from the senior center. Most people who lived in Buttonville were even older than Grandpa Abe. They'd once worked at the button factory and had never moved away, not even after the factory shut for good. It took some time to get all the walkers and wheelchairs through the Town Hall door. Inside, rows of long wooden benches faced a small stage. Grandpa Abe's cane tapped as he shuffled down the aisle. He slid onto the bench in the very first row. Ben frowned. Sitting in the front row at school meant you'd get called upon by the teacher and asked all sorts of questions, like *Do you want to read your report out loud?* or *Did the hamster eat your homework again?*

"Why are you standing there?" Grandpa asked as Ben blocked the aisle.

"I'm allergic to front rows," Ben said. He quickly sat behind his grandfather in row two.

The hall began to fill. The whole place was

atwitter as people greeted one another and shared the morning news. Ben didn't hear any mentions of dragon sightings. That was a relief.

"Hi." Someone nudged Ben's arm. A girl with long blond hair and bright green eyes slid onto the bench next to him. The girl was Pearl Petal, his new friend and co-apprentice. Her green apron bore the slogan: **YOU GET MORE AT THE DOLLAR STORE**. "What's going on?"

"I don't know," Ben told her. "We never have emergency meetings back in Los Angeles."

"Oh, we have them all the time. When the Food 4 Less Market ran out of ice cream right in the middle of a heat wave, people went berserk, so there was a meeting about that. When your grandfather's cat ate Mr. Mutt's koi fish, there was another meeting. Last week, Mr. Filbert forgot to take his memory pills and he didn't come home for dinner. The town went on a flashlight search. We found him cuddling with a raccoon in the park. He thought it was his cat!" She laughed so hard she snorted.

Ben looked around. No one was paying particular attention to him. This would be a good time to tell Pearl about the dragon. "Hey, Pearl," he said. "Last night—"

"Listen up!" a voice hollered. Everyone went silent as a woman hurried down the center aisle and climbed onto the stage. Her overalls were as red as a radish, nearly matching the color of her frizzy hair, which was held down by a baseball cap. When she put a megaphone to her lips, her voice blasted out with hurricane force. *"Can you hear me?"*

"Too loud!" everyone replied, fingers plugging ears. "Too loud!" A bunch of hearing aids shrieked in protest.

She set the megaphone aside and put her hands on her hips. "Very well. Now, let's get down to the business at hand. As you all know, I am Martha Mulberry, president of the Welcome Wagon Committee, and this is my lovely daughter, Victoria." She pointed to a girl sitting in a corner of the stage, reading a book. "Say hello to everyone, Victoria."

"Hello, everyone," Victoria said, not bothering to look up from her book. Her frizzy red hair was pulled into two pigtails set so high on her head they looked like rabbit ears. She was dressed in the same red overalls as her mother.

"It has come to my attention that we have an emergency," Mrs. Mulberry said. "This morning, as I was peering through my binoculars, checking on my neighbors, I noticed that Mr. Bumfrickle's garbage can was missing."

Pearl elbowed Ben. "A missing garbage can," she whispered. "Phew. I thought it was going to be something about Dr. Woo."

Ben had been worried about the same thing. "Uh, Pearl..." He scooted so close he could smell her peppermint gum. "Last night—"

"Attention!" Mrs. Mulberry clapped her hands, then continued her explanation. "After discovering the missing can, I began my morning walk so I could inspect the neighborhood. That's when I noticed that my mailbox was missing." She cleared

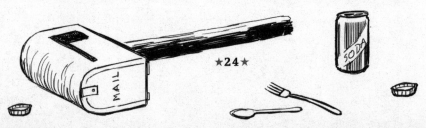

her throat. "Buttonville citizens, there is a thief in our midst."

Grandpa Abe stood and leaned on his cane. "My toaster's missing."

"I can't find my spatula," someone said.

"And I can't find my favorite fork."

"My watering can is gone."

The hall buzzed with voices as everyone began calling out missing items. All the items had one thing in common—they were made of metal. *How weird*, Ben thought.

Mrs. Mulberry clapped her hands for silence, then pointed a suspicious finger at the second row. "Pearl Petal? Are you the culprit?" Everyone turned to look at Pearl. She had a bit of a reputation as a troublemaker.

"Me?" Pearl scrambled onto the bench and stood as tall as she could, towering over the mostly gray-and white-haired audience. That's when Ben noticed Pearl's pink shoes. During their last visit to Dr. Woo's hospital, Pearl and Ben had met a leprechaun

who was being treated for a head cold. The leprechaun took a liking to Pearl and gave her the shoes.

"I didn't do it," Pearl said. "I already have a toaster and a spatula and plenty of forks. And why would I want a mailbox and a garbage can? That's ridiculous." Her parents, who were sitting in the front row, nodded in agreement. Pearl sat back down with a loud "*hmmph.*"

"If it wasn't Pearl, then who?" Mrs. Mulberry tapped her toe. "It seems odd that we have two new people in Buttonville, and suddenly, things start disappearing. One of those new people is Ben Silverstein. The other is Dr. Woo." She pointed again. "Do you know anything about this, *Ben?*"

"No," Ben said, swallowing hard. "I don't know anything. Zero. Zip. Nada." The back of his neck got all sweaty. "Absolutely nothing."

"That's right," Pearl said. "Ben knows absolutely nothing about those things disappearing."

Mrs. Mulberry cleared her throat. "Then there is only one conclusion to be made. Dr. Woo didn't bother coming to our emergency meeting because..."

She picked up the megaphone and said, "*Dr. Woo is a thief. I demand that she be arrested.*"

Ben's stomach went into a knot. Pearl grabbed his arm.

"We have to do something," she said. "We can't let them arrest Dr. Woo."

4

asps of shock echoed throughout the hall. And because many of the gasping people were very old, coughing fits followed. Mr. Mutt had to turn up his oxygen tank. Mrs. Froot had to be slapped on the back. Someone's dentures flew across the room.

"Settle down, everyone." The person issuing this order was Officer Milly. She worked for the Buttonville Police Force. She was also Pearl's aunt. Her polished black shoes squeaked as she walked onto the stage. Her police badge was so shiny Ben had to squint against the glare. She folded her arms and peered over the rims of her dark glasses at Mrs. Mulberry. "You can't accuse someone of committing a crime without proof. Do you have proof?"

"I may not have proof, but I have plenty of questions," Mrs. Mulberry said, smiling so big her gums showed above her teeth. "Question number one: Why did Dr. Woo move here? Question number two: Why did she open a worm hospital when no one in Buttonville has a pet worm? Question three: Why does she keep the gate to her hospital locked at all times?"

Ben and Pearl looked at each other. They knew the answers but didn't dare say anything. They'd signed contracts of secrecy, after all.

Mrs. Mulberry continued. "I believe Dr. Woo keeps her gate locked because she's the person who's stealing our things."

"A locked gate is not proof of anything," Officer Milly pointed out. "Have you been inside the hospital? Have you witnessed suspicious activity?"

"Ben and Pearl have been inside," Victoria Mulberry said as she looked up from her book. Her blue braces sparkled with spit. "They work at the hospital, so they'd know if Dr. Woo is stealing."

Ben fidgeted on the bench. Things were moving in a bad direction. But at least no one had mentioned a dragon.

Officer Milly slid her glasses down her nose and looked directly at Ben and Pearl. "Have either of you seen any of the stolen items inside Dr. Woo's Worm Hospital?"

"No," Ben and Pearl answered, which was the

one hundred percent truth. They'd seen all sorts of other stuff, like a leprechaun with a head cold, a sasquatch with foot fungus, and a redheaded man with a tail. But no missing toaster, spatula, garbage can, mailbox, or fork.

"Dr. Woo isn't a thief," Ben added so loudly that his voice echoed off the walls. He thought Dr. Woo was amazing. She'd given him two certificates of merit, which he'd tucked into his sock drawer. "She'd never steal. She's a nice person." Her dragon, however, was another matter entirely.

Mrs. Mulberry snorted. "How do we know she's nice? We've never met her."

"If my grandson says she's a nice person, then she's a nice person," Grandpa Abe said. He took off his canvas hat and pointed his cane at the stage. "You should live so long, Martha Mulberry, to be as nice a person as Dr. Woo."

"I want my questions answered," Mrs. Mulberry said with a stomp of her foot. "There's a thief on the loose. I demand that Dr. Woo come out of her worm

hospital and talk to us. And if she won't come out, then we'll force our way in."

A few heads nodded. Some people mumbled in agreement. Officer Milly took out a pad of paper and a pen. "There's no need to force your way into the hospital, Martha. I will handle the investigation. First, I need to make a list of the missing items."

As everyone else began to move toward the stage, Pearl motioned to Ben and he followed her up the aisle. "That Mrs. Mulberry is a pain in the rump," she said as soon as they'd stepped outside.

"Pearl, there's something I need to tell you." Ben closed the Town Hall door. "Last night—"

But Pearl wasn't listening. "What if Mrs. Mulberry forces her way into the hospital?"

"That would be terrible," Ben said. "If people found out Dr. Woo's secrets, she might have to leave. And then our apprenticeships would be over."

"Well, I'm not letting that happen." Pearl kicked a red button down the steps. "I'm going to find the thief and—"

Plop! Something bounced off Pearl's head. It was

a clump of moss that had rolled down the roof. Pearl furrowed her brow. "What was I saying?"

"You were saying that you were going to find the thief," Ben said. "But you don't need to, because—"

A scratching sound caught his attention. More clumps fell, landing on the ground around Pearl's and Ben's feet. "Do you hear that?" he asked. "It sounds like something's on the roof."

Ben hurried down the steps and onto the sidewalk so he could get a better view. Shielding his eyes from the sun, he scanned the moss-covered shingles. He'd expected to find a bird hopping around or a squirrel scurrying about, but there was no sign of anything. Then his gaze traveled up the clock tower. He took a sharp breath.

A large black shape was perched at the very top.

"Uh-oh," Ben said.

"What's the matter?" Pearl joined him on the sidewalk. "What do you see? Oh...wow!"

The dragon's eyes glowed like red lightbulbs. It gripped the tower's steeple with all four paws, balancing like an elephant on a circus platform.

Ben looked around. Luckily, everyone was still inside the hall, talking to Officer Milly. "Hey!" he called, waving. This was no time to be cautious. "Go away. Shoo. Before someone sees you."

The dragon ignored Ben. It leaned over and gripped the clock's rim with its front paws. The tower trembled. Then the dragon bit down on the clock's shiny minute hand.

"What's it doing?" Pearl asked.

"It's stealing things that are made of metal," Ben said.

With a shake of its head, the dragon ripped the hand free. Nuts and bolts sprang into the air, then bounced down the roof.

"Hey!" Ben yelled. "You'd better stop doing that!"

The dragon unfolded its wings and took to the sky, the prize clamped in its mouth.

"Wait a minute," Pearl said. "Does this mean...?"

"Yep," Ben said. "That's what I've been trying to tell you. The dragon is the thief."

"But that's the dragon that lives on the hospital

roof," Pearl said. "So if it's stealing things from Buttonville..." She lowered her voice. "That means Mrs. Mulberry is right. Dr. Woo is responsible."

"What are you looking at?"

Both Ben and Pearl cringed. Victoria Mulberry had sneaked up like a silent fart. After squeezing between them, she pushed her thick glasses up her nose and stared at the sky. The dragon was still in view, its wings flapping gracefully.

"Holy cow," Victoria said. "That looks like a dragon."

Ben laughed nervously. "What are you talking about? I don't see anything."

"Up there." Victoria pointed. The creature swooped in a circle, then disappeared behind the tall treetops that surrounded Buttonville. "That looked *exactly* like a dragon."

A story formed in Ben's mind. He was good at making up stories on the spot. It was like a super-power. "That was a helicopter designed to look like a dragon. It's a top secret project my father's working on. He's in military intelligence. You can't say anything about it or you'll compromise our nation's security." He tried to sound serious.

Pearl nodded. "Yep, that's right. Military intelligence."

Victoria scratched her freckled nose. "You're making that up," she said. "My mom told me your dad's a lawyer. She said your parents are getting a divorce and that's why you came to stay with your grandfather."

Ben hated that *d* word. He stuck his hands into his pockets and turned away.

"That's a rotten thing to say," Pearl told Victoria. "Why do you have to be so mean?"

Victoria frowned. "I'm just repeating what my mom said."

Pearl put her hands on her hips. "Maybe your mom should mind her own business."

"My mom says the truth is everyone's business."

"The truth? You want to talk about the truth?" Pearl's cheeks turned red. She stuck her face right up to Victoria's. "Well, guess what, *Victoria*? That thing *was* a dragon. A real fire-breathing dragon, and Ben and I know where it lives and you don't. So there." Pearl smiled triumphantly, revealing the big gap between her front teeth. Then her smile collapsed. "Oops."

Victoria's eyes got so wide behind her glasses they looked like they might pop out of her head. She ran up the Town Hall steps and burst through the door. "*Mom!*" she hollered.

"Drat," Pearl mumbled. "Guess I shouldn't have told her that."

"Of course you shouldn't have!" Ben's voice cracked. He appreciated the fact that Pearl had stood up for him—they'd only known each other for a few days—but why'd she have to spill one of their secrets? "We'd better go warn the doctor."

5

MOUSE CRACKERS

A tall wrought-iron fence surrounded the old building that had once been the Buttonville Button Factory. The sign hanging from the gate read:

WELCOME TO DR. WOO'S WORM HOSPITAL.

DR. WOO DOES NOT TREAT CATS, DOGS, PIGS, RATS, SNAKES, TURTLES, FISH, FROGS, OR ANY OTHER CREATURE THAT IS NOT A WORM.

DR. WOO SEES WORMS BY APPOINTMENT ONLY.

IF YOU DON'T HAVE AN APPOINTMENT,

KEEP OUT!

The entry gate was locked with a padlock, and the fence on either side of it had tips as sharp as swords. But down the sidewalk, behind a clump of trees, Pearl had discovered a section where the tips had rusted away. She and Ben quickly climbed over.

As they raced across the overgrown lawn, a few buttons crunched beneath Ben's sneakers. Pearl's legs were longer, making her a faster runner. Even though Ben was just as eager to tell Dr. Woo that her dragon was stealing things, Pearl reached the front door first.

A note taped to the door read:

Pearl pounded so hard the door rattled. Ben might have told her that it was rude to pound on someone's door, but this was definitely an emergency. "Hello?" she called. "Hello, hello?"

Ben fidgeted. He looked over his shoulder, fearing that at any moment a police car would drive up and park outside the gate, and Officer Milly would shout, "Attention, Dr. Woo, come out with your hands up. We know everything!"

Ben knocked. "Hello?" he called. "It's important. We need to—"

The sound of a dead bolt sliding open was followed by the sound of another dead bolt and another. Then a couple more. Five? During the last visit, they'd been told that a very dangerous person wanted to get inside the hospital. Five bolts seemed like a good idea, though they sure took a lot of time.

Finally, the door flew open.

A gentleman stood inside the hospital's entryway. The kids knew him as Mr. Tabby, the assistant to Dr. Woo. But on this day he looked different. Instead of his usual pressed trousers and vest, he wore a blue satin bathrobe and matching slippers. His long red hair was wound up in curlers, as was his mustache.

"Yes?" he asked in a peevish way, his yellow eyes narrowing. "May I help you?"

For a moment, Ben forgot why he and Pearl were standing on the hospital's front stoop. His attention was drawn to the box held in Mr. Tabby's hand. The label read:

MACKERS

MOUSE-FLAVORED CRACKERS

YOU'D HAVE TO BE WACKERS TO EAT ONLY ONE.

Mr. Tabby reached into the box and removed a square cracker that appeared to have a long, rubbery tail. Ben cringed as Mr. Tabby popped it into his mouth, slurping the tail like a spaghetti noodle. "Would you like one?" Mr. Tabby asked after licking his lips.

"No, thank you," Ben said. What he actually wanted to say was, "Eeew, gross."

"I'll take one." Pearl reached into the box and pulled out a cracker. She held it by the tail. "Uh, how come it's furry?"

Mr. Tabby ignored the question. "Why are you here?"

Ben was about to explain, but Pearl was quicker. "The dragon is stealing things. Lots and lots of things. Victoria saw it. She told her mom. Dr. Woo will get into trouble and—"

"What dragon?"

"The one that lives on the hospital's roof." Pearl pointed upward. "We know it lives up there. You don't have to pretend it doesn't. We've seen it flying around."

"Can we come in and talk to Dr. Woo?" Ben asked.

Mr. Tabby tapped his foot. "Are you aware that today is not a Monday, a Wednesday, or a Friday?"

"Yes," Ben said. "It's Tuesday."

"And are you further aware that you are only supposed to be here on a Monday, a Wednesday, or a Friday?"

Pearl bounced on her toes. "Yeah, we know, but—"

"Tuesday is my day off. My *only* day off." A low growl sounded in Mr. Tabby's throat. "Therefore, on Tuesday, matters regarding the Known World are not my concern."

Ben still wasn't used to hearing the term *Known*

World. That's what Dr. Woo and Mr. Tabby called the real world in which Ben and Pearl lived. There was also an *Imaginary World*, but neither Pearl nor Ben had been there.

"I bid you good day." And with that, the door slammed shut. The CLOSED note flapped as the five dead bolts slid back into place.

"Can't we talk to Dr. Woo?" Pearl hollered. There was no reply. She sighed. "I guess we'll have to wait until tomorrow. Unless..." She turned her green eyes upward.

"Oh no, I'm not climbing that rusty old fire escape," Ben said. "It's ten floors. We could fall." He had yet to brave the rock-climbing wall at his parents' country club, and it was only four floors high.

"But if we go up there, we can tell the dragon to stop stealing."

"I already tried talking to it, but it ignored me," Ben said. "I don't think dragons understand people language." There was nothing else to be done. They

couldn't tell Dr. Woo about the situation today, so they'd have to wait for tomorrow. "Besides, what if it's a mean dragon? They breathe fire."

"Yeah, okay." Pearl tossed the furry cracker into the grass. "I don't have time to climb a building anyway. I have to help my parents at the Dollar Store. We got a new shipment of socks from China."

Ben sighed. "Guess I'm stuck playing board games at the senior center." Though relieved he wouldn't be scaling the side of a building, he wasn't looking forward to spending time in that stuffy room filled with the scent of mentholated arthritis ointment.

Once they'd climbed back over the fence and were safely on the sidewalk, Pearl scrunched up her face as if she'd stubbed her toe. "I'm worried about getting into trouble." She spat her gum into a garbage can. "I told Victoria about the dragon. Does that mean I broke the contract of secrecy?"

Ben mulled this over. There'd been a lot of writing on the piece of paper they'd both signed. And

a lot of very small type. He hadn't read it all the way through. "I can't be certain, but I think you're safe. You didn't say anything about Dr. Woo, and you didn't say anything about her taking care of Imaginary creatures."

Pearl pulled a pack of Dollar Store gum from her pocket. She unwrapped a piece and popped it in her mouth. Then she handed one to Ben. "Do you think I'll get fired?"

"No," Ben said as he chewed. But the worried look on Pearl's face didn't go away. "Guess we'll find out tomorrow."

6

DOORKNOB DISASTER

At seven thirty Wednesday morning, Ben met Pearl in front of the Dollar Store. Pearl and her parents lived above the store, and her great-aunt Gladys lived in the basement apartment. The windows were decorated with all sorts of items you could buy for a dollar, from lightbulbs and lunchboxes to lemons and loofahs. Pearl was munching on a sandwich made from two waffles, scrambled eggs, and bacon. She loved turning her meals into sandwiches. "I'm super tired,"

she explained, her mouth half full. "I was up most of the night worrying."

"Me too," Ben said with an air-sucking yawn.

After leaving Pearl yesterday, Ben had played twenty-three games of checkers at the senior center. He'd purchased a new toaster at the hardware store. He'd eaten a dinner of leftover brisket and mashed potatoes and listened to his grandfather's stories about the good old days. Then he'd gone to bed. But every sound had drawn him to the window, searching the sky for the dragon. Snooze hadn't seemed concerned about the dragon's return. He'd waddled on his wheel and nibbled corn kernels. Barnaby, who'd eaten the dragon's scale, had slept peacefully. But for Ben, it had been a very long night.

Now he and Pearl were on their way to see Dr. Woo. They'd tell her what had happened and she'd know what to do.

As they walked down Main Street, they passed a lot of signs.

Many of the shops had gone out of business after the button factory shut down. The town looked like it was falling apart at the seams. Paint was faded, and lampposts had rusted. There were so many cracks in the sidewalk Ben decided he'd need wings or a jet pack to avoid stepping on them.

"Uh-oh," he said as he spotted red overalls and a red baseball cap a few yards away. Mrs. Mulberry, Officer Milly, and Ms. Nod, owner of the Buttonville Bookstore, were deep in conversation. Ben and Pearl stopped to listen.

"My knob is missing." Ms. Nod pointed to the

hole in the bookstore's front door. "Who would take a doorknob?"

"That's what I'm trying to figure out," Officer Milly said as she wrote on her little pad of paper.

"Another metal item," Ben whispered to Pearl.

"Why are you whispering?" Mrs. Mulberry asked, glaring at the kids. "What do you know about this?"

Pearl shoved the last of her breakfast sandwich in her mouth. Then, after a big swallow, she said, "Ben and I know nothing about this. Absolutely nothing."

"That's right," Ben said. "Nothing."

"I'm still convinced that Dr. Woo is behind these thefts," Mrs. Mulberry said with a stomp of her foot. "Let's go to the hospital right now and ask her all sorts of questions. I've made a list." She pulled a piece of paper from her pocket.

Officer Milly cleared her throat. "Have some patience, Martha. I'm in charge of this investigation and I will talk to *everyone* in town, including Dr. Woo. But it may take a few days."

"A few days?" Mrs. Mulberry threw her hands in

the air. "And in the meantime the thief will continue to steal. As president of the Buttonville Welcome Wagon, I take safety very seriously. I didn't sleep a wink last night, I was so worried. And my daughter's

such a nervous wreck that she's hallucinating. Yesterday she said she saw a dragon!"

Ben and Pearl looked anxiously at each other.

"We gotta go," Pearl said, tugging on Ben's sleeve. "Bye."

He followed her away from the bookstore. As soon as they were out of earshot he said, "Why would a dragon keep stealing metal?"

"Well, you can get money for metal at a recycling center," Pearl pointed out.

"Yeah, but why would a dragon want money?"

"Beats me." Pearl tucked her T-shirt into her orange basketball shorts. Her pink slippers didn't match her outfit, but who could blame her for wearing them? He wished he had a pair of leprechaun shoes—just not in pink. "Let's go."

They darted around the corner and bumped right into a red wagon that was blocking the sidewalk. "*Victoria*," Pearl snarled. Victoria Mulberry, who was sitting in the official welcome wagon, looked up from her book.

"I've been waiting for you," she said. She held out

an empty pickle jar. "Know what I got here?" She smiled proudly, exposing her glistening blue braces.

Ben leaned close to the jar. A little something lay inside. "It looks like a piece of spaghetti."

Victoria blinked. Her glasses were so thick they made her eyes look like they belonged on a frog. "It's not a piece of spaghetti. It's a worm. I found it.

Dr. Woo won't let my mom into the hospital unless she has a sick worm. This one's real sick. It's not even moving."

Pearl grabbed the jar and shook it. Then she snorted. "It's not moving, because it's dead."

"Dead?"

"It's all dried up." Pearl handed the jar back to Victoria. "Dr. Woo doesn't take care of dead worms. Too bad, *Victoria*." Then Pearl skedaddled up the sidewalk.

"You can't put a worm in a jar without dirt and water," Ben explained. "They need moisture."

Victoria's rump was wedged inside the wagon, so it took her a few moments to scramble to her feet. "My mom wants me to be an apprentice just like you and Pearl. But I think worms are gross."

"Ben," Pearl cried. "Come on or we'll be late."

Ben tried to get away, but Victoria stepped in front of him. "I saw that dragon," she said, spit flying from her braces. "I told my mom, but she didn't believe me. She said I was having a nervous

breakdown, and she made me take a nap. But I know what I saw. Tell me where it lives."

"Uh..." Ben shuffled. He felt his cheeks go red. "Uh..."

"Ben!" Pearl hollered. She'd made it to the next block.

"Bye," he said. Then he darted around Victoria.

"I saw it!" Victoria yelled. "I'm not crazy!"

As Ben ran after Pearl, he didn't know whom he felt sorrier for—Victoria or the worm. But there were more pressing matters—like protecting Dr. Woo and her dragon.

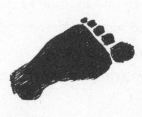

7

POOPER-SCOOPERS

A t 7:59, Ben and Pearl arrived at the hospital
gate. At eight o'clock on the dot, the hospital door opened and Mr. Tabby walked down
the long driveway. The curlers were gone and his
red mustache was expertly groomed into individual
segments, like whiskers. His black slacks were perfectly pressed, and his white vest, with red polka
dots, bore not a single stain. As his polished shoes
crunched against the gravel, a ring of keys jangled
from his fingertips.

"Why are you two bouncing around like kernels

of popcorn?" he asked after unlocking the gate.

"Because we need to tell you something." Pearl pushed the gate open, and she and Ben rushed through.

Mr. Tabby flexed his nostrils and sniffed. "Do I detect the odor of bubble gum?" He sniffed again. "Yes, indeed I do. Is it necessary for me to remind you, *Pearl*, that gum is not allowed on hospital grounds?"

"I forgot," Pearl said. Then she swallowed. "Sorry. It's gone now."

"Let us hope that will be the only rule you break today." Mr. Tabby narrowed his yellow eyes. "Well? What is it you *need* to tell me?"

"The dragon stole a doorknob from the bookstore," Ben said.

"And my aunt Milly's going to come here and ask questions. She's a police officer. We need to tell Dr. Woo."

"Dr. Woo is not on the premises." Mr. Tabby locked the gate. Then he walked up the driveway with Ben and Pearl at his heels.

"When will she be back?" Ben asked.

"She will be back when she returns." Mr. Tabby's strides were long and graceful.

"She will be back when she returns?" Pearl repeated. "That's like saying something will be over when it ends."

"Or we will get there when we arrive," Ben added.

"Exactly."

Pearl frowned. "If you're going to answer a question that way, you might as well say nothing at all."

Mr. Tabby's ears twitched. "That would be nice, indeed."

One of the things Ben had noticed about Dr. Woo's assistant was that he tended to lean on the grumpy side of life. He'd made it quite clear to the kids that he wasn't thrilled about their apprenticeships, because he didn't want to get stuck *babysitting* them.

"Mr. Tabby? Can I ask you something?" Pearl quickened her pace, trying to keep up as they neared the front stoop. "There's this girl named Victoria Mulberry. I don't like her, because she's super nosy and she never invites me to any of her parties. Anyway, yesterday I told her—"

"I am not interested in the conversation that took place between you and the human named Victoria," Mr. Tabby said.

"But—"

He turned on his heel and pointed a finger at Pearl. "The best *but*s are no *but*s." Then he twirled back around and opened the front door.

Pearl shrugged. "I tried to tell him."

Ben sighed with relief. He didn't want Pearl to get into trouble for talking about the dragon. He didn't want to be the only apprentice or, worse, share the job with Victoria Mulberry.

"Please secure the door," Mr. Tabby said to Ben once they were all standing inside the entryway.

Ben had neglected to lock the front door on his first visit to the hospital, and that was how the sasquatch had escaped. He was determined to never make that mistake again. "These bolts are huge," he said as he slid all five into place. "No one could get in here without a battering ram."

"A battering ram? Hmmmm." Mr. Tabby stroked his mustache. "I hadn't thought of that. Are they available in town?"

Pearl shook her head. "I don't think so. We've never sold any at the Dollar Store."

"Excellent. One less thing to worry about. Please follow me." Mr. Tabby crossed the lobby and pressed his fingertips against a door marked EMPLOYEES ONLY. The door hummed, then clicked open. They entered a hallway and walked straight for the bulletin board. Ben and Pearl grabbed their time cards from the OFF DUTY side of the board. Another card remained for someone named Vinny. They punched their cards through the time clock, then pinned them to the ON DUTY side, next to the one for Mr. Tabby and another one for Violet.

"Who are Vinny and Violet?" Pearl asked. She'd asked this before, and today she got the exact same response.

"Violet and Vinny work for Dr. Woo, and that is all you need to know," Mr. Tabby replied.

In the closet, Ben and Pearl found new lab coats. The last ones had gotten soaked with lake water and lake-monster slobber. Ben thought that the lab coat was the coolest uniform, so much better than the tan pants and maroon shirts he had to wear for school.

"What are we doing today?" Ben asked. While he'd spent much of the night thinking about the dragon situation, he'd also wondered what amazing creature they might see on their second official day as apprentices. It would be spectacular to meet a Pegasus or a griffin.

"As I recall, you've been instructed to give the sasquatch a flea bath," Mr. Tabby said. Ben groaned. He'd hoped they wouldn't have to deal with the stinky sasquatch again. But on Monday, Pearl had broken a rule by taking an Imaginary creature, the leprechaun, outside the hospital. The flea bath was the punishment.

"However," Mr. Tabby said with a flick of his mustache, "the sasquatch is currently napping. We have a steadfast rule—never wake a napping sasquatch

unless you wish to be flung to the very top of a tree. Do you have such a wish?"

Ben and Pearl shook their heads.

"Wise decision," Mr. Tabby said. "While we are waiting for it to arise, you can clean the roof."

"The roof?" Ben glanced at the ceiling. "But doesn't that dragon live up there?"

Mr. Tabby's half-moon eyes flashed. "Indeed, a dragon lives on the roof."

"Uh..." Ben's stomach tightened. "It's a pretty big dragon. Should we go up there? I mean, where does it rate on the danger scale?"

The danger scale was a system used by Mr. Tabby to rate Imaginary creatures. For example, a creature that nips at fingers might rate a level one. A creature that shoots poisonous venom from its eyeballs might rate a level four. But the most dangerous creatures of all, the ones that like to eat humans, rate level five. Because Ben and Pearl had very little experience with Imaginary creatures, they were not supposed to face a level four or five.

"The dragon that lives on the roof is a Western

black dragon. Most full-grown Western dragons are level five. The black variety is particularly nasty." A low growl vibrated in Mr. Tabby's throat. "Lucky for you, this dragon is young and rather tame. Well, tame-ish."

"Tame-*ish*." Ben gulped. "What does that mean?"

"That means he has promised to not eat peasants and to not set any villages on fire. That brings him down to a level two."

While two sounded so much better than five, Ben wondered if dragons were good at keeping promises. And since there weren't any "peasants" in Buttonville, did that mean the dragon could eat grandsons, senior citizens, and Dollar Store employees?

"Hey," Pearl said as she buttoned her lab coat. "I thought Imaginary creatures weren't supposed to live in the Known World. How come this one lives here?"

"This particular creature was saved by Dr. Woo when he was a hatchling. Because of his injuries, he stayed under her care for an entire year, and as a result, he imprinted."

"Imprinted?" Pearl asked.

"Dragons become attached to the first being who takes care of them. This dragon became attached to Dr. Woo and is loyal to her. He refuses to return to the Imaginary World."

"What about the baby dragon I found on my bed?" Ben asked.

"That hatchling wasn't in human company long enough to imprint. It was returned safely to the Imaginary World."

Mr. Tabby took out his creature calculator, a device he kept in his vest pocket. It contained all the information he needed about the creatures that were being treated at the hospital—the species and gender, the illness or injury, and the current location. "Our dragon appears to be gone at the moment, so you don't have to worry about disturbing him."

Ben's heart thumped a few extra times. The last thing in the world he wanted to do was to *disturb* a dragon.

"He's probably stealing more stuff," Pearl said. "He's going to get Dr. Woo in trouble."

"That is not your concern. Dr. Woo will tend to

such matters when she is able." Mr. Tabby reached
into the supply closet, then handed Ben a shovel
and Pearl a bucket.

"What's this for?" she asked.

Mr. Tabby's nose twitched. "For the collection and proper disposal of dragon droppings."

Both Ben and Pearl groaned. Pooper-scooper duty!

"You will take the stairs to the roof," Mr. Tabby instructed as he led them to the stairwell at the end of the hall. "Go straight there. Do not dally. Do not dawdle. And whatever you do, do not, I repeat, *do not* open the door to the tenth floor." He leaned over and put his face very close to Pearl's face. "The tenth floor is off-limits. Do you understand?"

"Of course I understand," Pearl said. "We speak the same language, don't we?"

Ben noticed the glint in her eyes. From the way she tried to hide her smile, he could tell she was already planning on sneaking a peek at the tenth floor. Well, he wasn't going to risk another sasquatch punishment. No way. "We understand," he told Mr. Tabby. "The tenth floor is off-limits."

Mr. Tabby straightened himself, then pointed to the stairwell. "Very well. Off with you."

That's when a voice boomed from a ceiling speaker. "Mr. Tabby to the Incubation Chamber. Immediate assistance required. The pixies are percolating. Repeat, the pixies are percolating." Ben and Pearl had heard this voice before. It was very nasal and monotone, as if it came from a computer.

"Oh dear," Mr. Tabby said as he checked his creature calculator. "What a predicament. I must go. Percolation is a matter of urgent importance." He dashed away. "You two are on your own," he called. The door leading to the lobby closed behind him. Its *thud* echoed down the long hall.

"I hope the sasquatch naps all day," Pearl said.

"Me too." Ben gripped the shovel. "We'd better hurry and clean the roof before the dragon comes back."

8

THE HOSPITAL ROOF

The stairs were steep. When Ben reached the seventh floor, his legs felt as if they'd turned to stone. "This is like climbing a mountain," he complained. Pearl, eager to get to the roof, scampered up each flight as nimble as a monkey, the bucket swinging from her hand. When Ben finally caught up, she was standing on the last landing.

"Floor ten," she whispered.

Ben leaned the shovel against the wall. "Don't… even…think…about…it," he said, gasping for breath. He pointed to a sign that was tacked to the door.

FLOOR 10

OFF LIMITS
DO NOT ENTER
STAY OUT

THIS MEANS YOU

Pearl pushed some wisps of blond hair from her eyes. "Oh, come on, Ben. Just a little peek. What harm could that do?"

"What harm?" His breath was wheezy. "You still want to keep this apprenticeship, don't you? Breaking another rule won't help, that's for sure."

"Drat! I guess you're right," she said, stepping away from the door. "I told Victoria about the dragon. I shouldn't do anything else that might cause trouble." She patted Ben's shoulder. "Thanks for helping me remember the rules."

Ben wasn't sure she needed help *remembering*. But she certainly needed help *following*.

There were nine steps remaining, and they led to a metal door. Pearl pressed down on the handle. As

the door swung open, fresh air streamed in, cooling Ben's sweaty face. But it didn't cool his nerves, which were sizzling with worry.

Without hesitation, Pearl stepped out onto the roof. Ben stayed in the doorway, his gaze searching for anything big, black, and fire-breathing. "The dragon's not here," Pearl reported. "You can come out."

Phew. But Ben's relief was followed by a twinge of embarrassment. How could Pearl be so brave?

The roof of the old button factory was flat and surrounded by a tall ledge. Dozens of chimneys poked up here and there. The south side looked out over the gravel driveway and the padlocked gate. Buttonville's clock tower rose in the distance. The north side offered a view of Button Lake and the surrounding forest. Morning sunlight glimmered on the lake's surface, but there was no sign of the lonely lake monster they'd met on Monday.

Ben sniffed, then looked down. A large glob sat at his feet. It looked like a slightly squished chocolate cupcake, only there were feathers and tiny bones sticking out of it. "I think I found a dragon dropping," he said.

"Yuck." Pearl set the bucket next to it. "Looks like he's been eating pigeons."

Ben scooped the dropping with the shovel, then plopped it into the bucket. "You keep watch while I clean," he told Pearl, since there was only one shovel. "Warn me if you see the dragon flying this way."

"Okay." She shielded her eyes with her hands and looked into the sky.

Things weren't so bad. At least the droppings weren't gooey, and they didn't smell half as disgusting as the sasquatch. Ben found two more, each full of feathers and bones. If the dragon had been eating people, Ben expected there'd be zippers, shoelaces, and jewelry in the poop. Fortunately, there were no signs of such items. Moving quickly, he made his way around the chimneys. Soon, the bucket was full. "Mr. Tabby said something about proper disposal. What do you think we're supposed to do?"

"We can't carry that stuff downstairs," Pearl said. "How gross." She grabbed the bucket. Before

Ben could stop her, she dumped the contents over the eastern wall. The grass below had grown into a weed-infested field. The droppings disappeared among the tall blades.

"Why'd you do that?" Ben asked.

"Now it's fertilizer," Pearl said with a smile. "That seems like proper disposal to me."

Ben shrugged. It was a clever idea, but he had a nagging suspicion Mr. Tabby would have a different opinion.

There was one last part of the roof to clean. Hoping with all his heart to finish before the dragon returned, Ben hurried around the largest chimney. Then he skidded to a stop. "Pearl...?"

She was at his side in a heartbeat. "Whoa! What's that?"

They both stared, slack-jawed, at the mess sitting before them.

It was a giant pile of stuff. And all the stuff was made from metal. Ben had to squint because the objects shone in the sunlight. "I see a hubcap, a mailbox, and a spatula," he said as they walked

around the pile. "There's a bunch of forks, a door-knob, and—hey, there's my grandfather's toaster."

"Look, there's the clock hand from Town Hall."

Just as Ben was about to grab the toaster, a shadow swept across the pile. "Uh-oh," he said. A very large shape flew right at them. "Run!"

Pearl, who'd been brave up until that moment, dropped the bucket and bolted across the roof. Ben, who didn't care about being brave but who cared a great deal about not getting eaten, dropped the shovel and ran as fast as he could. A thunderous sound followed as the dragon's wings beat the air above their heads. *Go, go, GO!* Ben's brain hollered. Two more chimneys and then the door. *Run, run, RUN!*

Swoosh. A gust of air blew past Ben. A loud *thump* was followed by the clattering of chimney tiles. The dragon had landed.

And he stood right above the exit.

9

DRAGON FOOD

Ben had never felt more terrified in his life. Nothing could compare to this—not the vampire film festival his dad had taken him to, not the torture chamber at the wax museum, not even the night at math camp when the counselor had told the zombie brain-sucker story.

The dragon's dramatic size took Ben's breath away. His black chest was as broad as Grandpa Abe's Cadillac. His red eyes glowed like they were on fire. He stood on four paws, towering over the kids, his claws digging into the roof like grappling hooks.

Pearl pressed against Ben, her whole body shaking as if she'd gotten very cold all of a sudden. "Ben," she whispered. "What should we do?" She grabbed his hand and squeezed.

"I don't know."

It was odd to see Pearl so scared. On Monday she'd faced the lake monster with confidence. But comparing that gentle, long-necked creature to this

seething fire-breather was like comparing a garter snake to a wolverine. Those claws alone could rip a car into pieces!

With a graceful leap, the dragon landed directly in front of Ben and Pearl. He opened his mouth, and a piece of metal fell out—the other clock hand from Town Hall. His upper lip curled, exposing a row of teeth that looked exactly like steak knives. Not only was each tooth serrated, but it was also crooked. Dr. Ruben, Ben's dentist, would have loved to get his hands on such a mouth. This dragon could be the poster child for orthodontists everywhere.

He growled.

Ben clenched his jaw, holding back a sound that might have been a squeal but might also have been a shriek—he couldn't be sure. His parents would be heartbroken if he got eaten. He could hear his grandfather's voice at the funeral, *"Oy gevalt!* Who would have thought such a thing could happen to such a nice boy?"

Ben and Pearl both took a step back, then another.

The dragon took a step forward, then another. Steam hissed from his nostrils.

Something had to be done. Immediately!

"H-h-hello." Ben's voice sounded very far away, as if it had gotten trapped in his throat. "We're sorry if we disturbed you. We were just leaving."

The dragon snorted. A flame shot out.

"Whoa!" Ben cried as he pulled Pearl sideways. Fortunately, the flame shot way over their heads and did nothing more than heat up the air.

Pearl clutched Ben's hand extra hard. "Please don't be mad. Mr. Tabby told us to come up here and clean up your..." She chewed on her lower lip. "Clean up your..."

"Don't say *poop*," Ben whispered from the corner of his mouth. "We don't want to insult him."

Suddenly, one of the dragon's front paws reached up, grabbed a pigeon right out of the air, and shoved it into his mouth. A couple of pigeon feathers floated to the ground.

"Gross," Ben said with a grimace.

"Totally gross," Pearl said.

The dragon chomped, then swallowed. Ben didn't want to think about the bird's fate. A dragon's stomach had to be a terrible place. "We work for Dr. Woo," he said, pointing to his lab coat. "We're the new apprentices."

The dragon brushed a feather from his snout and continued staring at the kids.

"I think you're right," Pearl whispered from the corner of her mouth. "Dragons don't speak people language. They're reptiles, and reptiles aren't very smart."

The dragon's upper lip curled. Then he sat on his haunches, pressed his front claws together, and did something amazing. "I wonder," he said in a voice so deep it rumbled like thunder. "Does an apprentice taste as good as a pigeon? Do you?"

He stared directly at Ben.

10

METALMOUTH

Did he taste as good as a pigeon?

Ben pondered this question. Firstly, he didn't know what pigeon tasted like. Maybe like chicken or Cornish game hen. Both were very delicious. Secondly, he was not about to compare himself to something delicious.

So he did what he did best. He made up a story.

"I taste terrible," Ben said. His hand slipped out of Pearl's grip. "As a matter of fact, I'm poisonous because I take all sorts of allergy medications. When I was a baby, I ate paint chips, so I have toxic levels of lead in my bloodstream. And I love junk food, so I'm full of chemicals and preservatives."

The dragon smacked his lips. He did not appear convinced.

"Plus, I live right next door to a nuclear power plant, so I'm radioactive. If you eat me, you'll get sick and die."

"Mmmmm," the dragon hummed, paying no attention to Ben's story. "To eat this apprentice or not to eat this apprentice? That is the question."

A long pause followed, during which Ben's life flashed before his eyes—but not the life he'd already lived. He saw images of things he'd been looking forward to. He saw himself lighting the menorah for the next Hanukkah and unwrapping eight days of presents. He saw his bar mitzvah party, where his friends would raise him up in the air during the horah dance. And he saw himself holding his brand-new driver's license. None of that would happen if he became dragon chow.

"*Ben!*" Pearl yelled from across the roof. With

the dragon distracted, she'd made it to the exit and was holding the door open, motioning for Ben to run. It wasn't as bad as the obstacle course in gym class, except for the fire-breathing dragon and the razor-sharp teeth. He'd simply have to duck beneath the dragon's elbow, dart around his right haunch, leap over his tail, then race straight for the exit. Pearl's ponytail bobbed as she waved frantically.

Ben sent all his energy to his feet, preparing to bolt, but the dragon burst into a smile. "Ha-ha. Just kidding."

Ben froze. "Huh?"

"I'm not going to eat you." The dragon was chuckling, and his voice had changed. It no longer sounded terrifying—it sounded like a little kid's voice. "But I scared you good, didn't I? Didn't I scare you good?" He thumped his tail. "That was my big mean voice."

Ben wasn't sure what was going on. Was this a joke? Was the dragon teasing his food before eating?

"Don't play with your food," Ben's mother always said.

The dragon smirked. "You should have seen the look on your face. Ha-ha."

Wait a minute. Ben narrowed his eyes. Mr. Tabby had said the dragon was young. The dragon was acting like a...kid.

"That wasn't funny," Ben murmured, hoping his heart would settle back to normal and Pearl wouldn't see the sweat that had broken out on his forehead. He'd been so scared he'd almost peed his pants!

Pearl sprinted around the dragon, then gazed up at him. She was smiling so wide you could see the gap in her teeth. "I can't believe you can talk."

His tail stopped thumping. "Of course I can talk. Dragons invented language."

Ben made a *phff* sound. "Invented language?" That sounded like a story, for sure.

"Yep. Way back in the Foggy Time. That's when the Imaginary World began. At least that's what my dragon book says." He reached between two scales and pulled out a book.

Then he opened the book to a page that was dog-eared. "This is me." He turned the book so Ben and Pearl could see. They stepped closer. The page had a drawing of a dragon with the words *Black Western Dragon, Vicious and Deadly.* "It says I'm not very nice." The dragon frowned. "Says I eat peasants, burn villages to the ground, and steal treasure. But I've never done any of those things." He tucked the book back under his scale. "Hey, wanna play fetch?" He pulled a tennis ball from between two more scales and dropped it at Ben's feet. His tail thumped.

Ben picked up the yellow ball. Was this actually happening? The dragon wanted to *play*? "He wants you to throw it," Pearl said with a nudge.

"Okay." So Ben threw the ball across the roof. The dragon grabbed it right out of the air.

"Aw, that was too easy," he complained. "Throw it as far as you can." His tongue hung out of his mouth. "Go on, go on."

Using every muscle in his arm, Ben hurled that tennis ball toward outer space. It soared over the north wall, arched over Button Lake, then began its descent. The dragon whizzed into the air. Pearl and Ben peered over the ledge. The dragon's belly skimmed the water as he grabbed the ball. When he landed back on the roof, he dropped the ball at Pearl's feet. "Go on, go on," he said, bouncing on his hind paws. Then he stopped bouncing and scratched his head. "Hey, I forgot to ask your names."

"My name is Pearl and this is Ben. We're Dr. Woo's new apprentices. What's your name?"

Using one of his claws, the dragon picked a fork from his teeth. "My name's Metalmouth."

Ben approved of that name. And he didn't feel scared anymore. This dragon was like an overgrown

black Labrador retriever. "So, is this where you live?" he asked.

"Yep. Until Dr. Woo moves again. She's moved four times since I was hatched."

"Four times?" Pearl frowned. "I've never moved. I've always lived above the Dollar Store. Say, how old are you?"

"Dr. Woo says that in human years I'm..." He counted on his claws. "I'm ten."

"Just like us," Pearl said.

Metalmouth tossed the fork and the clock hand onto the pile of metal objects. Ben and Pearl looked at each other. "One of us has to tell him to stop stealing," Pearl whispered. "I vote you do it."

Ben rolled his eyes. "Gee, thanks."

"You're welcome."

Ben stuffed his hands into his jean pockets. "Uh, Metalmouth? Some of the people in town are kinda mad that...well...how come you're taking all that stuff?"

"I'll show you." *Swoosh.* His wings unfurled. "Get behind me so you don't get burned."

Burned? The dragon opened his mouth. Ben and Pearl darted behind the left wing. While the rest of Metalmouth's body was covered in sharp scales, the wing's skin was smooth and stretched between bones like silk over a kite's frame. As they peeked around the edge, the dragon's chest expanded with a deep breath. Then a flame shot out of his mouth. Metalmouth worked the flame like a painter, brushing every inch of the pile until each object had melted. Then the flame subsided and he tucked his wings. "Ta-da."

"Wow," Ben said.

The pile was transformed. What had been a hodgepodge of items was now a perfectly smooth silver nest, gleaming in the morning sun.

"How come you used metal?" Pearl asked. "I have a nest collection at home, and those nests are all made of twigs and sticks."

"Do I look like a bird?" Metalmouth asked. "Birds make stupid nests. Birds collect, but dragons steal. Birds weave, but dragons solder. Seriously. A dragon's nest is a work of art." Then he yawned.

To Ben, the dragon's breath felt like the air inside the country club's sauna. "I'm gonna sleep now."

Metalmouth stepped into the nest. He turned around three times like a dog. Then he curled up and wrapped his wings around himself like a blanket. After closing his eyes, puffs of steam began to waft from his nostrils.

"Oh, isn't that cute?" Pearl whispered. "He's snoring."

Ben didn't think *cute* was the right word, but it was kind of cool to have watched a dragon make his nest. He looked around. "I guess we're done up here." While he collected the shovel, Pearl grabbed the bucket, and together they tiptoed back to the exit. "That was amazing," he said after they'd entered the stairwell. "We talked to a dragon."

"Totally amazing." She closed the roof door. "Do you think he'll stop stealing now that he's built his nest?"

Ben was about to say he didn't know, but the wall speaker buzzed. "Mr. Tabby to floor ten. Emergency code red," the nasal voice said.

"Floor ten?" Pearl's eyes widened. "I wonder what's happening."

"Mr. Tabby to floor ten immediately. Mister—"

The computerized voice was interrupted by a new voice. "Mr. Taaaaabby! Mr. Taaaaabby! Where are you?" the voice pleaded.

"Who's that?" Ben asked.

"I don't know, but it sounds like she needs help," Pearl said.

Ben gulped. Something bad was happening. "But Mr. Tabby is the one to help her. We're not supposed to—"

There was nothing to be done. Ben knew they weren't supposed to go to the tenth floor. The sign warned them not to go to the tenth floor. But the order came in, as clear as a bell. "Apprentices to Floor Teeeen!" the voice shrieked. "Now!"

11

GOAT LADY

The door on the tenth-floor landing opened into a vast room that stretched from one end of the building to the other. There was a floor, a ceiling, and some windows, but not much else. Except over in the far corner, where a woman sat on a stool, facing what looked to be an old-fashioned telephone switchboard.

Ben had seen photos of switchboards. In the olden days, people used telephones that were wired into the wall. This was before computers, so telephone operators physically connected the phone calls. They wore headsets and microphones and they'd say, "This is the operator. How may I place your call?" Then you'd tell them whom you were telephoning and they'd plug you into the right socket.

"Hello?" Pearl said. "We're the apprentices."

Without turning around, the woman motioned frantically. "Hurry up, y'all!"

Pearl and Ben started across the floor, Pearl in the lead as usual. Their steps disturbed a light dusting of yellow glitter. It appeared to be the same kind of glitter that always clung to Dr. Woo's clothing.

The woman was a bit too wide for the stool. Her blond hair was swirled like a soft-serve ice-cream cone on her head. The big red flowers on her dress matched her red high heels. She yanked off her headphones and spun around.

Pearl gasped. Ben gawked. The woman's face was strange indeed. Her nose started at the very top of her head. Her eyes were smallish and set far apart. She looked a bit like a goat, except she wore lipstick. *Don't stare*, Ben told himself, but he

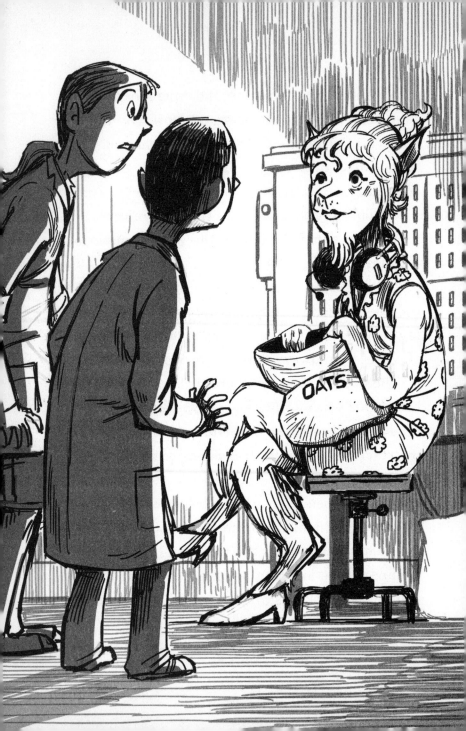

couldn't keep his eyes off her little goat beard. Then he noticed the goat ears sticking out of her hair.

"What took y'all so looooong?" she asked. She even sounded like a goat!

"We were on the roof," Pearl explained. "We got here as soon as we could."

"We're not supposed to be on floor ten," Ben said, nervously looking around. Was this a test of some sort? Would Mr. Tabby or Dr. Woo step out of the shadows and say, "Aha, you failed! You broke another rule"?

The lady reached into a burlap sack labeled IVY. She pulled out a long green vine and chewed. "My name's Violet," she said with her mouth full.

Ben glanced down. Violet's shoes were actually hooves, painted red, and her legs were covered in short fur. Was she half human and half goat? He'd seen creatures like that in a storybook but couldn't remember what they were called. She'd clearly come from the Imaginary World.

"We got ourselves an emergency caaaaall," she

explained as she reached into a bag labeled OATS.

"A call?" Ben stared at the switchboard, where an emergency light blinked. "Wait a minute. Are you saying you get *telephone* calls from the Imaginary World?"

"Well, of course." She stuffed a handful of oats into her mouth. "How else are we supposed to communicaaaaate?"

No good answer came to Ben's mind, because he didn't know where the Imaginary World *was*, exactly. Did it exist on Earth? On another planet? In another dimension?

Violet, the goat lady, stuck her head into the oat bag. Muffled chomping sounds emerged. She sure liked to eat.

Pearl fidgeted. "That red emergency light keeps blinking," she said. "Shouldn't we be doing something?"

Violet pulled out her head and snorted. Oats flew from her nostrils. "Dearie me, I almost forgot." Her hooves *click-clack*ed as she led them to a closet. She opened the closet door and pulled out a black leather satchel. "Dr. Woo isn't here, and Mr. Taaaabby is up to his eyeballs in percolating pixies. I can't leave the switchboard. You two'd better giddyup." She shoved the satchel into Ben's hands.

"Giddyup?" Ben's arms drooped under the bag's weight.

Pearl's eyes nearly popped out of her face. "Are you saying we get to go to the Imaginary World?" Her voice was so excited it bounced off the walls. "Seriously? Right now?"

"Well, of course right now, little darlin'. It's emergency code reeeeed." She patted the leather bag. "You'll find all sorts of medical supplies here."

"Medical supplies?" Ben gulped. "But we aren't doctors."

She blinked her small eyes. "Y'all are wearing doctor coats."

"Yeah, but that only makes us *look* like doctors. We're just apprentices. We can't—"

"We can," Pearl insisted. "We have certificates

in Sasquatch Catching and Curing Lake Monster Loneliness. We can do anything!" She yanked the satchel from Ben's hand. "Let's go!"

Ben wanted to go to the Imaginary World—there was no doubt about that. But how could he and Pearl be responsible for a creature that was injured? Sure, he could put a bandage on a cut, but what if the creature needed brain surgery, or a heart transplant? "I don't think—"

Pearl stomped her foot. "I want to go to the Imaginary World. Don't ruin this for me."

He wasn't trying to ruin anything. However, there were rules to follow. And there was a life at stake. "What kind of creature is hurt?" he asked. Violet didn't answer, because she was nibbling on Ben's sleeve. He pulled free of her tiny teeth. "Did you just eat my button?" She swallowed, then nodded.

"Don't get mad," Pearl whispered. "Goats eat everything."

Violet eyed Ben's other sleeve. He stepped away.

She picked an oat from her little beard and ate it. "Y'all watch the training video yet?"

"Training video?" both Pearl and Ben said.

"The one that tells you how to travel in the Imaginary Wooooorld."

Ben chewed on his lip. This sounded important. "No, we haven't watched it. I think we should."

"We don't need a video," Pearl said. "Just give me a map. I'm real good at following directions."

"There is no maaaaap."

Just then, the emergency button began to beep loudly. "Oh, dearie me. I don't know what to dooooo. No Dr. Woo, no Mr. Taaaabby. And two apprentices who don't know how to travel in the Imaginary World. There's nobody else heeeeere." She *click-clack*ed her way back to the switchboard and stuck her head into the oat sack again.

"Metalmouth is here," Pearl said.

Violet's head popped out of the sack. She looked at Pearl, blinked, then swallowed. "Why, little darlin', that's a dandy idea. He's been to the Imaginary

World. He can guide yooooou." She grabbed a micro-phone. "Metalmouth to floor ten immediately. Code reeeeed."

Pearl nudged Ben with her elbow. "This is great. Isn't this great? We get to go to the Imaginary World." Then she launched into her question-asking mode, firing them at rapid speed. "What do you think it looks like? Do you think it's beautiful? Is the sky green? Is there a sun and a moon or are there two suns and three moons? Do you think the plants are like the plants here or do they talk and sing? Is there—?"

Something crashed through the window. Pearl and Ben shielded their faces from shards of flying glass as Metalmouth soared across the room and skidded to a stop a few inches away. He had to hunch to fit beneath the ceiling.

"Why'd you wake me up, huh?" he asked. Then he yawned so wide Ben could see right down his throat.

"Y'all must go to the Land of Raaaaain."

Metalmouth rubbed sleep from his eyes. "Ah, gee-whiz, do we have to go now? I just built my nest."

"What's going on in the Land of Rain?" Ben asked.

"Well, I'm afraid it's real bad news." Violet the switchboard operator shook her head sadly. "The rain dragon is dyyyyying."

12

THE PORTAL

This much Ben knew—the creature was called a rain dragon and it lived in the Land of Rain. But it wasn't simply sick or injured—it was *dying*! And they were supposed to save it. He glanced at the black satchel. How could he and Pearl save a dragon's life when they'd had zero medical training?

"Shouldn't we wait for Dr. Woo?" he asked.

As Metalmouth yawned again, his steamy breath blew over Ben's head. "Yeah, let's wait."

"We can't wait, you guys. The rain dragon needs

help right now." Pearl squared her shoulders and gave Violet a determined look. "Tell us what to do."

"I like your spunky attitude, little darlin'. I can tell we'll get along just fiiiiine." Violet reached across the switchboard panel and pushed a large yellow button. A distant sound arose, thundering and crashing like an approaching storm.

"What's happening?" Ben hollered as the howling grew louder. Wind began to gather in the center of the room, whipping round and round, forming a mini tornado.

"That's the Portal," Metalmouth said. He scratched behind one of his horns. "I hate going in there."

"What?" Ben furrowed his brow. "We're supposed to go inside that tornado? Are you kidding? You're kidding, right?" Metalmouth shook his head.

"Cool," Pearl said. The swirling wind had kicked up the glitter, turning the tornado yellow.

"Wait a minute." Stories began to form in Ben's mind, reasons why he couldn't step inside a tornado and go to a place that had no map and that no one in his family had ever heard of. "My eardrums were

injured when I went scuba diving, so I'm not supposed to be in a tornado, or any kind of windstorm."

Violet made a little bleating sound. Then she handed a small glass vial to Ben. "Keep this safe. Don't lose it. It's your only way to get back heeeeere."

Ben gently cupped the vial as if it were a newborn baby. It was filled with yellow glitter. "The *only* way?" This was sounding more dangerous by the second.

A huge smile spread across Pearl's face, as if she were about to go to Hawaii. But this wasn't a vacation—this was a trip to another dimension. Her lab coat flapped against her basketball shorts. "Let's go!" She hurried to the center of the room, slipped into the tornado, and disappeared from sight.

"Ah, gee, do I have to go?" Metalmouth complained, his ears drooping.

Violet reached between two of his scales and pulled out the tennis ball. "Fetch!" she called as she tossed the ball at the tornado. Metalmouth's tongue hung from his mouth. The room shook as he bounded into the Portal.

"Shouldn't we take umbrellas if we're going to the Land of Rain?" Ben asked. He was stalling, of course. "We're supposed to be back by three o'clock. We can't—"

Lightning zapped. The Portal turned bright white. "Well, what are you waiting for?" Violet asked Ben. "It's gonna leave without yooooou."

Without him? Against every ounce of his better judgment, Ben ran straight into the light.

Wind swirled round and round. Howling filled his ears. Pearl's hair whipped and stung Ben's face. Metalmouth's scales prickled through Ben's lab coat. The storm sounds intensified. Thunder bellowed. Pearl grabbed Ben's hand, both their palms equally sweaty. She smiled at him. He couldn't smile. His face was frozen in an expression of utter terror. He gripped the vial in his other hand. The *only* way back.

There was a steadfast rule in Benjamin Silverstein's house—you must always tell someone where you were going. Even if you were walking down the street to visit a friend. His parents had no idea he was going to a strange land. If he didn't return, they wouldn't know where to look for him!

Suddenly, everything went black.

13

THE PORTAL'S PILOT

Ben stood in blinding darkness, his heart pounding. Pearl squeezed his hand so hard he could feel her pulse beating as fast as his own. What would happen next? Would they be shot through a wormhole? Flung into outer space? Turned inside out?

A little bulb flicked on, floating above Metalmouth's head. The bulb cast a dim glow throughout the Portal. The tornado had widened, creating a small room within. While the wind continued to swirl outside, the space inside became calm and quiet.

"What do we do now?" Ben asked the dragon.

Metalmouth spat out the tennis ball. "We gotta wait for the captain."

The captain?

"Welcome to the Portal," a squeaky voice said. Both Ben and Pearl jumped. Ben could have sworn that only the three of them had entered the tornado. Where had that voice come from?

Pearl released Ben's hand. "Who's that?" she asked.

"This is your captain speaking. Destination, please."

Metalmouth sat on his haunches. "We gotta go to the Land of Rain," he said.

"Setting course coordinates now. Fasten your seat belts. Prepare for takeoff."

"Seat belts?" Ben asked. "But we're standing."

The floor began to vibrate. Then, suddenly, the Portal shifted. Ben and Pearl tumbled against Metalmouth. "In case of a water landing, life jackets are located beneath the seat cushions. In case of a sudden loss in altitude, oxygen masks will fall from the ceiling." The captain's voice was super high-pitched, as if it belonged to an insect.

The tennis ball rolled back and forth during the bumpy ride. Ben grabbed hold of Metalmouth's leg to steady himself. "Whoa," Ben said as he almost tumbled over. The motion grew more turbulent. Ben felt like a sock inside a dryer.

Metalmouth groaned. "I don't like the Portal," he said. "It always makes me feel sick."

Ben didn't feel so good, either. And Pearl's face was turning an odd shade of green. "How long will this take?" she asked.

The captain didn't reply. Ben's head filled with dizziness. His stomach clenched. Metalmouth groaned louder. Oh no! Were Ben and Pearl about to experience *dragon vomit*?

Just when Ben thought he was going to lose it, the captain cleared his throat and announced, "Destination ahead. Prepare for landing."

The Portal leveled and the vibrations stopped. Except for Pearl's fidgeting, Ben's anxious breathing, and a dragon belch, all was quiet. What now?

The tornado continued to swirl around the perimeter of the Portal. An exit light appeared. "We would like to thank you for flying with us today," the captain's voice said. "We hope you will choose the Portal for your next interdimensional journey. Please refrain from pushing as you disembark."

Wow, it had taken only a minute or so to travel to the Imaginary World. It had taken Ben three hours to fly from Los Angeles to Buttonville.

"Come on," Pearl said. She picked up the black satchel and headed toward the glowing EXIT sign. Although Ben was no longer being tossed around, his heart was pounding in overdrive. What would they find once they stepped outside?

Metalmouth collected his tennis ball, tucked it behind a scale, then followed Pearl. They disappeared through the swirling wind, leaving Ben alone. Had his feet been glued to the floor? Why wasn't he following?

"Please proceed to the exit," the captain's voice said.

Ben realized he'd been gripping the vial of fairy

dust so tightly his hand was throbbing. Violet the switchboard operator's words echoed in his mind.

Only way home.

Metalmouth stuck his head back through the tornado. "Hey, Ben, whatcha doing? Huh? Whatcha doing? Are you scared?"

"No," Ben lied.

"Don't be scared. It's okay, Ben. Come on out." His red eyes twinkled.

Ben carefully tucked the vial into his pocket, hoping that his mom and dad wouldn't wake up tomorrow morning to the following newspaper headline: BENJAMIN SILVERSTEIN, AGE 10, DISAPPEARED MYSTERIOUSLY AFTER TRAVELING TO ANOTHER DIMENSION WITHOUT ASKING HIS PARENTS FOR PERMISSION.

If Pearl could do this, he could do this.

After checking to make certain the vial was safe, he stepped through the wind.

14

THE LAND OF RAIN

The Portal disappeared. No more tornado, no more swirling glitter. Nothing. Just Ben, Pearl, and Metalmouth standing in the middle of...

The Land of Rain?

It looked like a wasteland, as far as the eye could see. No trees, no shrubs or greenery whatsoever. The ground had hardened so that it was as dry and cracked as the heels of Grandpa Abe's feet. A ridge lay on the horizon. It looked to be made of dirt. Nothing grew on it. Had the entire place been colored with the same brown crayon? Even the cloudless sky was an odd tinge of brown.

"Are we in the right spot?" Pearl asked as she looked around.

Metalmouth shrugged. "I dunno. I've never been here before."

"What?" Ben's mouth fell open. "But you told us you've been to the Imaginary World."

"I have. Lots of times. I've been to the Valley of Fog and the Magnificent Marsh, but I've never been to the Land of Rain."

"If this is the Land of Rain," Pearl said, "then whoever named it has a weird sense of humor." Indeed, it looked as if rain had never fallen on this place. Not even a single drop. Pearl set the black satchel at her feet. Then she folded her arms and pouted. "I thought the Imaginary World was going to be exciting, with all sorts of weird stuff, like purple trees and flowers the size of houses. And three moons in the sky. But there's nothing here but dirt. Where are the unicorns and fairies?"

"Unicorns and fairies don't live in the Land of

Rain," Metalmouth said with a snicker. "Everybody knows that. They live in the Tangled Forest."

While it would have been interesting to learn about a forest filled with fairies, Ben was more eager to finish their assigned job and return safely home. "We need to find the rain dragon," he said. "It's dying, remember?"

"Where is it?" Pearl asked with a shrug.

"Guess we'd better start looking," Ben said. He and Metalmouth began to walk in one direction. Pearl, however, headed in the opposite direction. "Hey!" Ben called. "Where are you going?"

"We'll cover more territory if we split up." The satchel swung from her hand.

"I don't think that's a good idea," Ben said. "I think we should stay together. What if something goes wrong?"

Pearl stomped across the parched ground until she was standing right in front of Ben. "How come you're such a worrywart?"

He cringed. "I'm not a worrywart. I'm just trying to be logical."

"We have a better chance of finding it if we go in opposite directions," Pearl argued.

"Yeah, but..." Ben looked to Metalmouth for support. The dragon, who was batting the tennis ball between his paws, was paying no attention to the debate. "But you've got the medical bag and I've got the vial of fairy dust. If I find the rain dragon, I won't have any bandages or medicine. And if you get lost, you won't have any fairy dust for the Portal."

"I'm not going to get lost," Pearl said confidently. "I *never* get lost." Then she glanced at the satchel. "But you're right about the medicine. I guess we'd better stay together."

Ben turned his face toward the brown sky. A brilliant idea popped into his head. "Hey, Metalmouth, maybe you can spot the dragon from the air."

Metalmouth *thwapp*ed his tail. "Oh goody, I love flying." He began to gallop, the ground cracking beneath his huge paws. His black wings unfurled as he picked up speed. They flapped, but he didn't lift off the ground. He tried again and again. "Aw, gee, this isn't fair," he said. "There's some kind of magic here that's not letting me fly."

Ben sighed. "Guess we'd better start walking."

"What about that book?" Pearl asked. "Do you think it might tell us how to find the dragon?"

Metalmouth reached behind a scale and pulled out his book *History of Dragons* by Dr. Emerald Woo. He handed it to Pearl. The kids sat side by side, and Metalmouth stretched out on his belly as if about to be read a bedtime story. Pearl turned the pages. "Hey," she said, pointing to an illustration. "This looks just like you."

Indeed, the drawing was of a black dragon with glowing red eyes and enormous outstretched wings. The caption read: *Danger! Do not approach! The black dragon burns villages and eats humans!*

Metalmouth peered over Ben's shoulder. "That's a big, fat lie," he said with a snort. "I'd never do anything like that." His steamy breath tickled Ben's neck.

"I know just what you mean," Pearl said. "Lots of people call me a troublemaker, but that's not fair, because I don't *always* make trouble." She shrugged. "Well, not on purpose." She turned the page. Metalmouth gasped. The next illustration showed some angry villagers swinging rakes and swords at a black dragon.

"That's too scary," Metalmouth said as he held a paw over his eyes.

Pearl searched through the book until she found a drawing with the caption *The rain dragon.* "Oh, look, isn't it pretty?"

Metalmouth dropped his paw. Then he rested his chin on top of Ben's head so he could get a closer look at the book.

The dragon in this drawing was totally different from a black dragon. Its four legs were attached to a very long green snakelike body. The tail was feathered, and the horns were shiny and silver.

"How come it doesn't have wings?" Metalmouth asked.

Ben read from the opposite page. "'The rain dragon is a type of Chinese horned dragon. Horned dragons are the most respected of all Eastern dragons. The rain dragon is a female. Though wingless, she uses magic to fly. More than one cannot exist at the same time. Her sole purpose is to make rain.'"

"She's a girl. And she *makes* the rain," Pearl said. "Then that explains why the ground is parched. She can't make rain if she's dying."

"Listen to this," Ben said, continuing to read. "'While Chinese horned dragons vary in size, the rain dragon is vast and stretches for exactly two miles from the tip of her tail to the top of her snout.'"

"Two miles?" Pearl scrambled to her feet. "If she's that big, it should be easy to find her. We just need to get a better view. Maybe we can climb to the top of that ridge." Pearl grabbed the satchel and began to march across the cracked ground, her ponytail bouncing. When Ben and Metalmouth caught up, she was standing at the end of the ridge. "I can't get a good grip," she told them with a groan. "These leprechaun shoes are too slippery. Will you give me a boost?" Metalmouth cupped his front paws together. Pearl stepped inside, and he lifted her as high as he could. She scrambled up the last few feet.

"What do you see?" Ben asked.

Standing on tiptoe, Pearl reported her findings. "Well, this is definitely where the ridge begins. But it goes on and on and on as far as I can tell. I don't see anything else."

What terrible news. How were they supposed to help the rain dragon if they couldn't find her? Frustration took hold of Ben's thoughts. What would happen if they failed and the dragon died? Would there never be rain in the Imaginary World? Ben leaned against the ridge.

It moved.

The ridge...*moved.*

Having lived in Los Angeles all his life, Ben knew what earthquakes felt like. This hadn't been an earthquake. He pressed his hand against the ridge. It twitched. "I think I found our dragon," Ben said with a smile.

Pearl slid back down to the ground, landing beside Ben. Upon closer inspection, they discovered

that what had looked like a mound of dirt was actually the rain dragon's tail. "But she's supposed to be green," Pearl said.

"I wonder if she changed colors because she's sick." This was a reasonable guess, Ben thought. "Now we know we're not too late. She's still alive."

"Well, we're standing at the wrong end," Pearl said. "We'll have to walk two miles to reach her head."

But Ben had a better idea. "Hey, Metalmouth, can we ride on your back?" He was fairly confident he could hang on. After all, he'd taken riding lessons at his parents' country club.

"You got a saddle?" Metalmouth asked. Pearl and Ben shook their heads. "Then no can do. My scales will stab right through your clothes if you try to sit on me."

So they walked. And walked. And walked.

To keep Metalmouth from complaining about being bored, Pearl threw the tennis ball. To keep Pearl from getting tired, Ben and Pearl took turns carrying the black satchel. Without a cloud to

hinder it, the sun beat down. The heat didn't seem to bother Metalmouth, who pounced on the ball like an overgrown puppy. But sweat droplets gathered along Ben's collarbone. He felt sticky all over.

They followed the rain dragon's tail as it thickened, moving toward her hind legs. Cracks in the ground spread in all directions. Some were so wide Ben and Pearl had to jump over them. A few were so deep Ben couldn't see to the bottom. They'd stop every once in a while and touch the rain dragon. Ben was checking to make sure she was still alive. Pearl was letting her know that help was on the way.

"How much longer do you think we have to walk?" Pearl asked.

Ben had no idea. He didn't do much walking back in Los Angeles. He knew that Olympic athletes could run a mile in under four minutes. He tried to come up with a formula, but it was too hot to do math. "An hour," he guessed.

Pearl ran a few steps, then leaped over the widest crack yet. Ben stopped at the edge and looked down.

If he fell inside, how would he get out? Metalmouth had easily made the crossing and was chasing after his ball.

"Just get a running start," Pearl said from the other side. She smiled with encouragement. "You can do it."

Ben took a deep breath. He didn't want Pearl to think he was scared, so he pushed all his cautious thoughts aside and started to run. But he didn't get quite enough power behind the leap, and his foot slipped. "Aaah!" he cried, realizing he wasn't going to make it. The gap loomed, dark and endless as a black hole. He clawed at the air, desperate for something to stop his fall.

Pearl's arm shot out and grabbed the collar of Ben's lab coat. She yanked with all her might. They both tumbled to the ground. While Pearl landed on her backside, Ben landed in a face-plant.

"You okay?" she asked. "That was close."

Way too close. Ben got to his knees. His legs felt wobbly. He spat out some dirt. "Thanks," he said.

Then he looked into Pearl's green eyes. "You…you saved my life."

"You think so?" She pushed a few stray hairs from her eyes. "It was no big deal. I mean, you'd do the same for me."

No big deal? Ben swallowed hard. Without Pearl, he'd be lying at the bottom of that crevasse. "Of course I'd do the same for you." There was an awkward moment of silence as they looked at each other. Ben didn't know what else to say. But he did know that he'd never forget what had happened.

As Pearl wiped dirt off her knees, Ben got to his feet. Something made a clinking sound. The vial of fairy dust had tumbled from his pocket.

Before he could grab it, the vial rolled toward the crevasse and disappeared over the edge.

15

The vial of fairy dust was *gone*!

With a strangled cry, Ben fell to his knees and reached into the crevasse, his hands frantically searching the cold, dank air that lay below the surface. Then he lay on his belly, reaching farther, hoping the vial might have landed on a shelf, or that the crevasse wasn't as deep as it looked.

"You find it?" Pearl asked, crouching beside him.

"No," Ben said with a moan. "Metalmouth, can you help us?"

Metalmouth dropped his tennis ball and bounded over. "Lemme try." He also lay on his belly. Then he stretched out his arm, just as he'd done through the kitchen window to get Grandpa Abe's toaster. "Can't find it," he reported.

"Drat," Pearl said. She sat on the black satchel. "That's too bad. I dropped my house key down the drain. But we got a new key at the hardware store."

Panic started in Ben's toes and rose up into his throat. "What are we going to do?" he cried.

"Don't worry," Pearl said. "The goat lady knows we're here. She'll tell Dr. Woo, and then Dr. Woo will come get us." She looked at Metalmouth. "Isn't that right?"

The dragon sat up and scratched behind his ear. "Maybe. But Violet only works the day shift. If Dr. Woo gets back late, she won't know we're here until tomorrow morning."

"Tomorrow?" Ben imagined his grandfather waiting outside the hospital gate at three o'clock, wondering what had become of his grandson. He wiped sweat from his brow. There was no one to blame but himself. If he'd kept a tight grip on the vial, they wouldn't be in this predicament. Could they survive the night without water? Without blankets or shelter? And would his grandfather remember to feed Snooze?

Pearl checked the rain dragon's status. "Her skin feels colder," she said with alarm. "We can't sit here and worry about ourselves. We have a life to save."

She was right. Ben had made a terrible mistake, but there was still a job to be done. There was only one rain dragon in the universe, and she needed their help.

As they followed the dragon's body, Ben and Pearl tried to stay in Metalmouth's shadow. He didn't seem bothered by the temperature. Ben's mouth turned dry. When they arrived at the dragon's hind leg, they climbed over it. As they continued their journey alongside the dragon's mid-section, Ben's throat became so parched it felt like it was made of sandpaper. He tried not to imagine the cans of cream soda in his grandfather's refrigerator.

"I'm so thirsty." He opened the satchel, hoping to find water, but only found bottles labeled BLISTER LIQUIFIER, WOO'S WOUND GLUE, and TAIL AND TENTACLE DETANGLER.

"I'm thirsty, too, but I'm not drinking any of this stuff," Pearl said as she picked up a vial labeled SYRUP OF SERPENT SPIT. "Gross."

Metalmouth scratched under his chin. "How long can humans go without water?"

"Not long," Ben said. "Especially because we're sweating so much."

"Then why don't you just stop sweating?"

"We can't," Pearl said grumpily. "It's how our bodies keep cool."

"Human bodies make no sense," Metalmouth said. "You have no scales to protect you. And those patches of fur on your heads make you look super weird."

Ben guessed it was noon because the sun hung directly overhead. But maybe the sun had different rules in the Imaginary World. Sweat gathered between his toes. His socks were going to reek!

"You know what I'd like?" Pearl said. "I'd like an ice-cold vanilla milk shake. Or a root beer with extra ice. Or—"

"That's not helping," Ben grumbled. Would they

die of thirst before Dr. Woo came to rescue them?

The rain dragon's midsection was much shorter than her tail, so it wasn't long before they arrived at her front leg. They were about to climb over it when Metalmouth sniffed the air. "I smell metal."

"Metal?" Ben looked around. "I don't see anything made of metal. Are you sure?"

"Of course I'm sure." He thumped his tail. "Where is it? Huh? I want it!"

"Hey, guys!" Pearl had walked alongside the leg and had disappeared around the dragon's bent elbow. "You'd better come and see this!"

Metalmouth bounded forward, Ben at his heels. They both skidded to a stop next to Pearl. Ben's mouth fell open in astonishment.

The rain dragon's paw was caught in a trap.

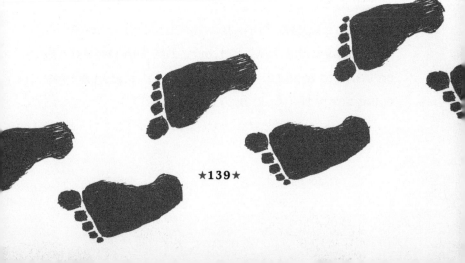

16

METAL TEETH

The trap looked like a pair of metal dentures that belonged to a giant. Grandpa Abe wore dentures. He kept them in a glass beside his bed at night, since he didn't need to chew while sleeping.

"Poor thing," Pearl cried as she and Ben raced toward the paw. "This is why she isn't moving."

A heavy chain was attached to the trap at one end and to a metal post at the other end. The post was hammered deep into the ground.

"Who did this?" Ben asked.

Metalmouth crouched real low, his ears folded forward. "Do you think it was a bunch of angry peasants?" He nervously glanced around. "Maybe I should get out of here."

Ben felt worried, too. Protecting Metalmouth from a rake-wielding mob could be tricky. And Metalmouth couldn't fly away to escape. Nor could they summon the Portal, because they no longer had the vial of fairy dust.

"Hey, you guys, come help me." Pearl was yanking on the trap with all her might. "We have to free her." Pearl was right. They'd worry about angry peasants later.

Even with the three of them working together, pulling and grunting like weight lifters, the trap didn't budge an inch. Then Ben had an idea. "Metalmouth? Couldn't you use your flame, like you did back on the hospital roof, to melt the metal?"

"That's a real good idea. Stand back." As

Metalmouth took a deep breath, Ben and Pearl scampered behind his wing, as they'd done before. A flame shot at the chain, cutting through it like a saw until the links broke apart. Then he aimed his flame at the corners of the trap, cutting a precise line around the hinges. The top half of the trap toppled over, landing on the hardened ground with a loud *clang*.

They watched, waiting for the rain dragon to get up and fly away. "How come she's not moving?" Pearl asked. "She's free."

They walked around the paw, examining it as best they could. The rain dragon had five toes, unlike Metalmouth, who had four toes. The trap had made indents in the paw, but none of the metal teeth had pierced the thick skin, so there were no wounds to tend to.

"She's still not moving," Pearl said.

"Something else must be wrong." Ben started walking. "We need to get to her head so we can talk to her."

"Uh-oh." Metalmouth stood on his hind legs and sniffed the air. "I smell something else."

"Is it water?" Pearl asked. "Please tell us it's

water." She and Ben looked up at Metalmouth, waiting for the word they longed to hear. A word that was clear, crisp, and drinkable.

Metalmouth sniffed again. Then he bared his jagged teeth and growled.

"What's wrong?" Ben asked.

He growled louder. The scales along his spine stood straight up, like the hair on the back of a cat. Ben's own spine got all tingly as a creepy feeling ran up it.

"What do you smell?" Pearl asked.

"I smell...*dragon blood*."

"Blood? That's why she's not moving," Pearl said. "She must have another injury. Come on!"

Despite their thirst, the trio picked up the pace. It only took a few minutes before they reached what looked like a forest. After referring to the drawing in Dr. Woo's book, they realized they'd arrived at the dragon's mane, which was made of feathers, each one as long as a pine tree. The feathers had also turned a drab shade of brown.

Metalmouth sniffed the air. "The scent is stronger."

"Look!" Ben pointed to a narrow stream that trickled along the cracked ground. But it wasn't filled with refreshing cool water—the liquid was thick and green.

"Dragon blood," Metalmouth said.

The blood boiled like porridge on a stove. Bubbles popped to the surface, then spat in small bursts. A splatter hit one of Ben's sneakers, burning a hole in the canvas.

"Watch out," Pearl said, dodging another splatter. They darted past the blood stream and kept hurrying until they reached the dragon's head.

A head the size of a house.

"Wow," Pearl said.

Ben stood in awe. He forgot about being thirsty. No words could express his amazement. Nothing in the Known World could compare. Even Metalmouth, who was as large as an elephant, stood in silence, dwarfed by the immensity of this other dragon.

The rain dragon's eyes were closed. Blood dripped

down her forehead and onto the ground. That's when Ben realized they'd found the source of the green stream. His heart sank.

One of her horns had been cut from her head, leaving behind a big, gaping hole.

17

THE RAIN DRAGON

They'd discovered the reason for the giant metal trap. It had held the rain dragon in place so that someone could take one of her horns.

"Who would hurt such a beautiful creature?" Pearl's eyes filled with angry tears.

"A hunter," Ben guessed. But what kind of hunter lived in the Imaginary World? Was it a person or another creature? "Maybe the rain dragon's horns are valuable, just like an elephant's or a rhinoceros'. Poachers kill animals for their horns."

"That's mean," Metalmouth said.

"This is the most horrible thing I've ever seen. I wish my aunt Milly were here. She'd put whoever did this in jail."

Puzzled, Ben chewed his lower lip. Why hadn't the hunter taken both horns? Maybe it was easier to take one at a time since each horn was bigger than a refrigerator. "Whoever did this might come back," he realized. The hairs at the base of his neck electrified at the thought of facing someone or some-*thing* capable of such brutality.

Metalmouth covered his own horns with his paws. "I wanna go home."

Pearl patted his leg. "It's okay. Don't worry. We won't let the mean old hunter hurt you. I promise."

How can she make such a promise? Ben thought. They knew nothing about the Imaginary World and the creatures that lived here. But her words had seemed to put Metalmouth at ease, because he lowered his paws and nodded.

Feeling very sweaty, Ben took off his lab coat and laid it on the ground. Then he cupped his hands around his mouth and hollered up at the rain dragon. "Who did this to you? Hello?" The dragon didn't reply. Nor did she open her eyes.

"She's a Chinese dragon," Pearl said. "Do either of you speak Chinese?" Both Ben and Metalmouth shook their heads.

Another drop of green blood rolled down the dragon's face and landed near Ben's feet. "She might not understand us, but we need to stop that bleeding," he said.

"You're right." Pearl searched the black satchel and found an odd assortment of circular, triangular, and star-shaped bandages. "Drat! These aren't big enough."

"Hey, what about this?" Ben grabbed a bottle he'd seen earlier, the one labeled WOO'S WOUND GLUE. "It might help."

"Dr. Woo used that stuff on me when I stepped on a fork," Metalmouth said. Ben figured he'd been *stealing* the fork at the time. "My toe's as good as new." He held out his left rear paw and wiggled the third toe.

"We'll have to climb."

"Climb her face?" Ben thought this sounded like a very rude thing to do.

"We're so small she probably won't even notice," Pearl said. "But Metalmouth should stay down here. He's way too big. His claws might hurt her."

"I don't wanna stay down here alone." Metalmouth's ears collapsed, and he wrapped his tail around himself. "What if the poacher comes back? Huh? What if?"

It struck Ben as odd that such a big creature could look so afraid. But he didn't blame Metalmouth one bit. Clearly this poacher was ruthless and cruel. "Just use your big mean voice," Ben said. "The one we heard on the hospital roof. It scared me."

"Me too," Pearl said.

Metalmouth nodded. Then he raised himself onto his hind legs, unfurled his mighty wings, and said, "You mean THIS VOICE?" His eyes flashed, and a flame shot out of his mouth. Even though Ben knew it was an act, a jolt of fear ran down his legs. Metalmouth sat back down and smiled. "Like that?"

"Yeah," Ben said with amazement. "Just like that."

Pearl took off her lab coat and tied it around her waist. After a boost from Metalmouth, Ben and Pearl stood on the rain dragon's upper lip, right in front of her snout. Ben had expected steam to seep out of the cave-sized nostrils, but her breath was cool. It felt like air conditioning. Ben raised his arms and let it waft over his body.

Pearl sighed. "That feels so good," she said.

The skin between the nostrils was creased, so it formed little steps. They walked up the nose, then stood on its crest, looking up at the forehead. Luckily, the slope was gradual and the terrain remained rutted, making it easy to grip, even for Pearl's pink slippers. The rain dragon's eyes were still closed—each eyelash as thick as rope.

"We're walking on a dragon's face," Pearl whispered. "I bet you've never made up a story this good."

He hadn't. The whole day had been the most amazing story ever. A goat lady, a tornado, and not one but *two* dragons. If the Portal reappeared with Dr. Woo inside, then it would be a happy ending. But if they never saw the Portal again—that was a story Ben didn't want to tell.

When they reached the dragon's brow, they took a quick look around. The desert stretched on and on as far as they could see. It appeared they were all alone. No hunters. No poachers. No Portal. Ben waved at Metalmouth. Metalmouth waved back.

After a bit more climbing, Pearl and Ben rushed over to the hole. It was the size of a plastic kiddie swimming pool. Green blood bubbled up and out, too hot to touch.

Ben uncorked the bottle of wound glue. He hesitated. "Do you think we're doing the right thing?" he asked. They'd had zero medical training. They didn't even know if this particular dragon had allergies to medication.

Pearl patted Ben's shoulder. "Go ahead. Metalmouth said it worked for him."

Ben held out his arm and poured until the bottle was empty. The green puddle sizzled and popped, then stopped moving. A dark film began to form, just like the skin on cooked pudding. In a matter

of seconds, the wound had sealed and the bleeding had stopped.

"Yay!" Pearl cheered. She hugged Ben. "I knew we could do it."

Ben smiled. Yes, they'd done it. His face flushed with pride. But what would happen next? They peered over the crest of the dragon's brow. Her eyes were still closed.

"Why isn't she waking up?" Pearl asked. "We stopped the bleeding." But the rain dragon lay perfectly still. "Shouldn't she be doing something? Like making rain?" They both glanced up at the sky. The sun was shining. No clouds had appeared.

"Is she still breathing?" Ben asked.

They slid down her nose. Pearl stood in front of a nostril, but her hair didn't billow, nor did her basketball shorts ripple. "I can barely feel her breath," she said. "She's still alive. But do you think...?" She spun around and looked at Ben, her eyes wide with fear. "Do you think we're too late?"

It was a very sad thought indeed. They'd freed her

paw, they'd closed her wound, but if the rain dragon had lost too much blood, what else could they do?

"Look!" Pearl grabbed Ben's arm and pointed. "What's that?"

Shielding his eyes with his hands, Ben squinted toward the horizon. Something was out there. Because the sun had dropped lower in the sky, Ben couldn't get a good look at the shape. But whatever it was, it was definitely moving toward them.

Was the poacher coming back?

"Crud," Ben mumbled.

As quickly as they could, he and Pearl leaped onto the dragon's upper lip, then jumped to the ground. "Metalmouth," Ben said, "someone's coming this way."

Metalmouth spat out his tennis ball. "Uh-oh." He began to turn in a circle. "We gotta get outta here. We gotta hide."

"We can't abandon the rain dragon," Pearl said.

Ben's instinct was the same as Metalmouth's. Running and hiding would have been the best way to avoid danger. But Pearl was right. "If the hunter is coming back for the other horn, the rain dragon will die for sure," Ben said. "She can't lose any more blood."

Metalmouth stopped and cocked his head. "I don't want any dragon to die."

They all turned and squinted into the sun. The shape moved closer and closer.

"You know what to do," Ben said.

"Yeah. Big mean voice." Metalmouth reared up on his hind legs. As he opened his mouth, sunlight glinted off his jagged teeth. "Go AWAY!" he bellowed, steam hissing from his nostrils.

The shape moved toward them at a very brisk pace. Ben could now see that it was walking on two legs. And it was carrying something.

Metalmouth stepped in front of Ben and Pearl and raised his wings. *"Do not come any closer or I will eat you!"*

"If you eat me, then who will help you floss your teeth?" a voice asked.

Metalmouth smiled and *thwapp*ed his tail. Both Pearl and Ben also smiled.

For they could now clearly see the person hurrying toward them. She wore a white lab coat and carried a black medical bag.

"Dr. Woo!" they both cried.

18

RETURN OF THE RAIN

Ben felt relieved at first. Dr. Woo would have fairy dust, and she'd be able to take them back to the Known World. But when he saw the look on her face, he wanted to run in the opposite direction.

The doctor's long black hair swayed as she marched toward them. Her white lab coat was unbuttoned, billowing behind her like a sail. She stopped a few feet from them, set the black bag on the ground, then folded her arms and glared at her apprentices. "What is the meaning of this?"

"Uh-oh," Metalmouth said. He stepped behind Ben, as if trying to hide.

Stories began to pop into Ben's brain—stories that might keep Pearl and him from getting into trouble. But on this occasion, when a life was at stake, the truth seemed best. "The goat lady called us to the tenth floor," he began to explain. "And even though we knew we were breaking a rule, we—"

Dr. Woo held up a hand to silence him. Her index finger was missing. Ben had assumed that she'd lost it dealing with some sort of dangerous creature. The scars that ran across her cheek and down her neck were other indications that her job came with great risks. "Firstly, she is not a goat lady. She is a satyress, and her name is Violet."

"Sorry," Ben said. "Violet the satyress told us to—"

Dr. Woo held up her hand again. "Secondly, you have broken more rules in a single day than any other apprentices I have ever employed." She pointed at Metalmouth. "And you should know better."

Metalmouth's ears collapsed. Then he hid his head behind a wing.

"Do you have any idea how dangerous it is to travel through the Portal without proper training? Do you know how terrible it feels to get Portal travel sickness? Or to fall out of the Portal between dimensions? What would I have told your parents?"

Pearl took a cautious step forward. "Dr. Woo, we only came here because no one else could. You were busy and Mr. Tabby was busy, and Violet said the rain dragon was dying. We couldn't let her die."

"That's right," Ben said. Though he hadn't wanted to take this trip in the first place, now that he'd seen the rain dragon's injuries, he was glad Pearl had talked him into coming. "She needed our help. She still needs our help."

"Someone hurt her," Pearl said. "On purpose."

Metalmouth lowered his wing. "A hunter."

Dr. Woo sighed. "Tell me everything that has happened."

Ben explained how they'd found the metal trap and freed the paw. Pearl explained how they'd climbed up and poured Woo's Wound Glue into the hole. "She stopped bleeding, but she doesn't seem better," Pearl said. "She's barely breathing."

Dr. Woo removed a small device from her lab coat pocket. It was another creature calculator, identical to the one Mr. Tabby carried. She punched a few buttons and read the screen. "You did an excellent job with the wound glue. The rain dragon's physical health status has returned to normal."

"Then why isn't she moving?" Pearl asked.

"I don't know for certain, but I have a theory. You see, Chinese horned dragons are very gentle creatures that live in harmony with the universe. The rain dragon is the most gentle of all. She does not eat flesh—she eats clouds. She does not make war—she brings rain that keeps the valley lush. She does not argue, insult, blame, envy, or lie."

"Does she steal treasure?" Metalmouth asked.

"No," Dr. Woo said. "She does not steal."

"But if her health has returned to normal, why isn't she making rain?" Ben asked.

Dr. Woo put the calculator away. "Rain dragons are very proud of their horns. They are among the most beautiful in the Imaginary World. She feels the loss of her horn very deeply."

"Won't it grow back?" Ben asked.

"Antlers grow back," Dr. Woo explained, "but, alas, horns do not."

It occurred to Ben that the rain dragon's horn was one of many things that had been taken during the last couple of days. His grandfather's toaster had been stolen, but it was easy to buy a new one. Same for new forks, garbage cans, and mailboxes. This horn, however, was special. How could it possibly be replaced?

"Poor thing," Pearl said. "She feels so sad. How can we make her feel better?"

"I know how to lance boils, how to stitch snouts and mend broken tails, but I'm not very good at fixing feelings," Dr. Woo said.

Ben looked up at the rain dragon, his gaze resting on the remaining horn. It wasn't white like Metalmouth's horns. It was silvery and glistened in the sunlight. And its surface was so smooth it could have been made of...

"Metalmouth?" Ben said, an idea flitting around in his head.

"Yeah?"

"Remember that chain link that was attached to the trap?"

"Uh-huh."

"Do you think you can melt that into something else? The way you melted all that stuff and made your nest?"

"Sure."

"Oh, Ben," Pearl said, her eyes twinkling. She

grabbed his arm. "That's an amazing idea!"

While Pearl and Dr. Woo stayed with the rain dragon, Ben and Metalmouth ran back to the dragon's paw. Using his flame, Metalmouth separated one of the chain's links from the others. Then Ben wrapped the tip of Metalmouth's tail around the link and Metalmouth dragged it back to the rain dragon's head.

As the others watched, Metalmouth melted, melded, shaped, and soldered a beautiful silver horn. It was a work of art, just like his nest.

Ben, Pearl, and Dr. Woo carried the horn up the rain dragon's face and set it carefully on top of the hole. The doctor used an adhesive specifically designed to reattach horns. "It should hold for at least a thousand years," she said.

The ground shuddered.

"She's moving," Pearl said.

Just as the rain dragon opened her eyes, Ben, Pearl, and Dr. Woo slid down her nose and jumped onto the ground. The dragon raised her head. After batting her long lashes, she reached up with one

of her paws and touched the new horn. The edges of her mouth turned upward.

"She feels better," Dr. Woo said.

Then all at once, the dragon's body bloomed with color. It was as if someone had used a giant eraser on her. All the brown disappeared. Her skin turned lime green, her mane buttery yellow, her eyes tangerine orange, her whiskers ocean blue. She was a living rainbow.

The dragon lifted her neck and gazed down upon them.

"We must show her our respect." Dr. Woo placed her palms together and bowed. Ben, Pearl, and Metalmouth did likewise. The rain dragon bowed her head. Then she exhaled a long string of clouds.

"Wow," Metalmouth said. "I wish I could do that."

The clouds floated above their heads, blocking the sun. The air immediately cooled. Ben took a long, refreshing breath. His sweat was gone. Even his sunburn disappeared. Metalmouth's scales glistened with dew.

The rain dragon extended one of her claws and drew something in the hardened ground. It was a symbol, and it looked like this:

Ben had seen it before, but he didn't know what it meant.

Then she took to the sky, her long, snakelike body gliding in S-shapes and circles. The clouds sighed and let loose their rain. Drops the size of golf balls fell onto the parched ground. Ben wiped water from his eyes. Pearl tilted her head and opened her mouth.

"I'm drinking imaginary water," she said. "And it tastes great." Ben drank some, too. Metalmouth lapped from a puddle.

The strange symbol disappeared as the ground turned to mud. Then newborn shoots began to sprout. In a few minutes, what had been a dry wasteland was transformed into a lush carpet of greenery. Ben was soaked all the way through to his skin,

but he didn't care. As rain rolled down his face, he thought only of the amazing sight above him—a wingless dragon, looping and gliding across the sky.

"Our work here is done," Dr. Woo announced. She reached into her coat pocket and pulled out a vial of yellow fairy dust.

"Wait," Pearl said. "Shouldn't we find out who took the rain dragon's horn? My aunt Milly knows how to check for fingerprints. Maybe we could borrow the equipment from her."

"There is no need. I already know who took the horn." She sprinkled some dust in the newly sprung grass. "Step back."

The tornado appeared as it had on the tenth floor, swirling and thundering. Ben wasn't afraid this time. He didn't need to be pushed or convinced. He stepped right in.

19

ANGRY VILLAGERS

Thank you for flying the Portal. Please refrain from pushing as you disembark."

Ben, Pearl, Metalmouth, and Dr. Woo stood on the tenth floor of the old button factory. Puddles formed around them as water dripped off their clothing. Metalmouth shook like a dog, spraying the walls and ceiling. There was no sign of Violet the satyress. The yellow light on the switchboard had stopped blinking. The bags of oats and ivy were gone. The shattered glass had also been cleaned up, and the window replaced with a new one.

"Who took the rain dragon's horn?" both Pearl and Ben asked as the last wisps of tornado disappeared.

Dr. Woo set the extra medical bag into the closet. "His name is Maximus Steele. He's not supposed to be in the Imaginary World, but he's apparently found a way to get in." She closed the closet door. Pearl opened her mouth, about to ask a million questions, but Dr. Woo gently silenced her with a raised palm. "Maximus Steele is a very dangerous man." Dr. Woo's wet hair clung to her cheeks and neck. Water leaked from the pockets of her lab coat. "If you continue to work as my apprentices, I will tell you all about him. But right now, there is another important matter to attend to."

Ben's sneakers squeaked as he and Pearl followed the doctor over to the windows. He'd noticed how she'd said, "*If* you continue to work as my apprentices." Was she still angry that they'd broken the rules? Was she going to fire them?

The windows offered a bird's-eye view of the front of the hospital. Two people stood at the gate. Ben recognized the red overalls of Mrs. Mulberry and her daughter, Victoria. The little red welcome wagon sat beside them. "It appears we have angry villagers at our door," Dr. Woo said.

"Angry villagers?" Metalmouth backed up into the corner. "I don't like angry villagers. Make them go away." His legs began to tremble. Ben was certain he was imagining all those horrid drawings from the dragon book.

"They're mad about the missing stuff," Ben explained. "But they're not going to hurt you. Don't worry."

"I needed to build my nest," Metalmouth said. "I can't sleep without a nest."

"You are quite right," Dr. Woo told him. "A dragon must have a nest. This is my fault, not yours. I should

have provided you with the necessary materials." She tapped her four-fingered hand on the window-sill. "If they ask too many questions, I'm afraid we'll have to move again."

"Don't do that!" Pearl cried.

"We could buy new stuff for everyone," Ben said. "That would make them happy."

Dr. Woo smiled sadly. "While that's a nice idea, I'm afraid I have little time to spare."

What could they do? Ben had only known Mrs. Mulberry for a few days, but he could tell she was the sort of person who wouldn't give up easily. She wanted to prove that Dr. Woo was the thief. If only they could give Mrs. Mulberry something to make her happy. Then she might stop trying to get inside the hospital.

Ben smiled as a brilliant idea just about knocked him off his feet, like the stink of a sasquatch. "What if Metalmouth made something? Something out of metal. He could give the town a present." Ben didn't want to hurt Pearl's feelings, since she'd lived

there all her life, but Buttonville was as run-down as a town could get. It could use something pretty. "What do you think?"

"Where would he get the metal?" Dr. Woo asked.

"I know," Pearl said. "The trap is still in the Land of Rain. And the chain links. He could use those."

"Excellent," Dr. Woo said.

Metalmouth groaned. "Ah, gee, do I have to go back through the Portal?"

"Yes," she told him. "But be quick. I have no time to deal with angry villagers." Then she led the kids to the door.

"Dr. Woo?" Pearl asked. "What did the rain dragon draw in the dirt?"

Dr. Woo leaned against the doorframe. "That is called yin and yang. It is the ancient Chinese symbol of opposites. Man and woman, day and night, plus and minus—the universe is composed of opposing energy. The rain dragon was letting you know that while there are bad humans

there are also good humans. While there are hunters who take horns, there are also Ben Silversteins and Pearl Petals who put them back." She smiled at them. "I am very proud of both of you."

"Really?" Pearl said.

Ben beamed. He'd expected a reprimand, or at the very least, a terrible sasquatch chore.

"Yes. Really." But Dr. Woo's smile was short-lived. Her expression turned serious once again. "Though you handled yourselves cleverly under difficult circumstances, do not make a habit of traveling to the Imaginary World without me. I would hate to lose both of you." Then she glanced at her wristwatch. "You'd better hurry up with that flea bath. It's nearly three o'clock in the afternoon."

Right. The sasquatch still needed a bath. Ugh.

As they stepped out onto the tenth-floor landing, Metalmouth called, "Hey, Ben!" Ben turned around. "This is for you." With a nudge of his snout,

Metalmouth sent the yellow tennis ball rolling across the floor. It knocked into Ben's sneaker. Ben picked it up. Despite the fact that it was soaked in dragon slobber, he was happy to have it. He tucked it into his pocket.

20

FLEA BATH

It didn't turn out to be as difficult a chore as Ben had imagined. He and Pearl were already soaking wet. While Ben sprayed the sasquatch with a hose, Pearl squirted it with liquid soap. Then they scrubbed it with wire-haired brushes. All sorts of things fell out of its fur—twigs, moss, rocks, grasshoppers, and some drowned fleas. When it was rinsed clean, Ben and Pearl toweled it dry. The sasquatch seemed to like the attention. It even admired itself in a mirror when the bath was over.

Pearl and Ben put everything away in the supply closet: the bucket and shovel from pooper-scooper duty and all the flea bath equipment. They tossed their wet lab coats into the laundry bin and punched out with their time cards. As they stepped into the lobby, they nearly bumped right into Mr. Tabby. His perfectly creased trousers were wrinkled, and his vest had little holes. His mustache was drooping, and he was pinching something between his fingers. It looked like a tiny insect.

"This should be the last one," he said as he dropped it into a jar, where it wiggled and buzzed. Then he screwed a lid in place, trapping the creature. "Pixies," he grumbled. "I hate it when they percolate."

Pearl and Ben tried to get a better look at the creature, but Mr. Tabby shoved the jar into his vest pocket. "It is three o'clock, time for you to leave. I understand you broke many rules today." His nose twitched. "And it has come to my attention that you did not dispose of the dragon droppings in the correct manner."

Ben gave Pearl an "I told you so" look.

"Therefore, when you return on Friday, your punishment shall be..."

Ben gritted his teeth. What now?

"...to trim the sasquatch's nose hairs to a precise quarter-inch length."

Pearl giggled. "That's going to be totally gross."

"Why do we have to keep doing things with the sasquatch?" Ben asked.

"Every creature that comes to us for care is important," Mr. Tabby said. "Never forget that." Then he reached into another pocket and pulled out two pieces of paper, each rolled and tied with string. "Dr. Woo asked me to give you these certificates of merit, for helping with the rain dragon."

Ben and Pearl took their rewards. After unbolting and opening the front door, Mr. Tabby looked down the driveway. Mrs. Mulberry was peering through the gate with a pair of binoculars. Victoria was sitting in the red welcome wagon, reading. "I expect you'd like to avoid those two?" he asked.

"Yes," Ben and Pearl both said.

"I will distract them." He stepped out onto the front stoop and waved at Mrs. Mulberry. She let go of her binoculars and waved back.

"Yoo-hoo!" she hollered. "Hello there! Yoo-hoo!"

Mr. Tabby began to walk down the driveway, very slowly. "Good afternoon," he called. "How may I help you?"

Mrs. Mulberry jumped up and down with excitement. Victoria never looked up from her book.

Crouching real low, Ben and Pearl darted into the tall grasses. As Mrs. Mulberry clung to the bars of the gate, hollering, "We want to come inside!" Ben and Pearl sneaked across the side yard and climbed over the hidden section of fence. When they were safely on the sidewalk, they waved at Mr. Tabby.

He stopped walking. "You wish to come inside?" he asked Mrs. Mulberry.

"Yes."

"Do you have a sick worm?"

"No."

"My dear lady, this is a worm hospital. If you do not possess a sick worm, then I bid you good day." And with that, he turned briskly on his polished heel and hurried into the hospital, where he immediately shut and bolted the door. Victoria ignored the entire scene, her nose buried in her book.

"Hey!" Mrs. Mulberry called, shaking the gate. "Come back! I have unanswered questions!"

Pearl and Ben snickered.

"That was the most amazing day yet," Pearl said. They stood behind a clump of trees, safely hidden from view. "Can you believe we climbed up a dragon's face?"

"Don't forget about traveling to another dimension," Ben added.

"I'll never forget any of it. I'll remember every single moment for the rest of my life." She pulled a pack of gum from her pocket and handed a piece to Ben. The wrapper was soggy, but the stick was perfectly chewable. "I'm wondering..." She chewed for a bit. "Remember what Mr. Tabby had said about a dangerous person trying to get inside the hospital? Do you think that could be Maximus Steele?"

"I hope not," Ben said. He glanced over at the building. Someone who could trap a rain dragon would probably find it easy to get past five dead bolts. "And I hope we never meet him."

Pearl took off her slippers and twisted each one, wringing them dry. Then she slid them back onto her feet. "Well, if I ever meet him, I'm going to dispose of dragon droppings right on his head!"

Ben chuckled. He had no doubt she'd do just that.

Pearl started across the road, in the lead as usual. But it didn't bother Ben this time. He'd come to realize something. That yin and yang was true.

For every girl who sought adventure, there was a boy who was cautious. And that was perfectly okay.

Just as they reached the first intersection, Grandpa Abe pulled up and offered to drive Pearl to the Dollar Store. They both climbed into the backseat.

"*Oy vey*, why are you two soaking wet?" Grandpa Abe asked.

As Ben fastened his seat belt, a story filled his mind.

PUT YOUR IMAGINATION
≡ TO THE TEST ≡

The following section contains writing, art, and science activities that will help readers discover more about the mythological creatures featured in this book.

These activities are designed for the home and the classroom. Enjoy doing them on your own or with friends!

CREATURE CONNECTION
⋆ *Chinese Horned Dragons* ⋆

China is one of the oldest civilizations on our planet. And one of the most popular characters in Chinese mythology is the dragon.

While the dragon in Western countries is war-like and aggressive, the Chinese dragon is peaceful, friendly, and wise. It is a symbol of power, strength, and good luck, which is why the emperors of China chose the dragon as their symbol.

There are many types of dragons in the Chinese tradition, but the dragon that Ben and Pearl encounter in the Land of Rain is a horned dragon. This type of dragon has been given an unlimited amount of power by Chinese storytellers. It can become as large as the universe or as small as a worm. Although it has no wings, it can fly through the sky or through water. It can breathe clouds that make storms and produce rain.

The life cycle of the horned dragon is long and

complicated. It can take a millennium (a thousand years) for the dragon to go from a hatchling to a mature adult. After age 500 it is called a scaled dragon. After age 1,500 it is called a lung dragon. Between ages 1,500 and 2,000 it grows horns. The dragon in our story must be very old indeed.

If you are lucky enough to visit a Chinese dragon, it will bestow on you many gifts, for these dragons are generous creatures. You are extra lucky if you find a real dragon bone. Tradition claims that if these bones are ground into powder and eaten, the person doing the eating will live for a very long time.

While the Chinese horned dragon gets along with most creatures, including man, there is one it fears— the tiger. This is why the tiger and the dragon appear on opposite sides of the Chinese zodiac wheel.

One of the questions scientists ponder is—did dragons exist? We have skeletons proving that dinosaurs and woolly mammoths once roamed the earth, but no one has ever found a dragon skeleton. And it seems unlikely that a creature could breathe fire. But the question remains—why are ancient stories about these creatures found in civilizations all over the world? In a time when people couldn't communicate over long distances, the same descriptions and drawings were being created by storytellers who lived continents apart.

And so we still wonder—is it possible they were real?

So the next time you see something large flying across the sky, and you think it might be an airplane, take a longer look. You never know.

STORY IDEAS

Imagine that you are the emperor of China. News has reached you that a dragon has been found, living peacefully in the hills above the empire. You are old and very sick. And you know that dragon bones can bring you long life. But you also know that to harm a dragon could bring bad luck to your empire. What do you do?

★ ★ ★ ★ ★

You are a horned dragon and your job is to make rain. All day long you fly around, breathing clouds and summoning storms. You're getting kind of bored with the same old routine. Then one day, you run into another dragon who has an entirely different job. What is it? And what happens when you trade?

ART IDEA

Draw a dragon—any kind of dragon. Go for it! Give it horns. Give it scales. Make its body snakelike or make it fat. Give it whiskers or a beard. Are there wings? That's your choice. Maybe it has two sets of legs or four. The dragon comes from your imagination. Color it red, yellow, green, blue, or all the colors in the rainbow. Have fun.

CREATURE CONNECTION
★ *Satyrs* ★

The ancient Greeks created a vast collection of stories that centered on many gods. These are known as myths. One of their lesser gods was called Pan. He was an odd-looking fellow. His lower half was goat, and his upper half was human. And sticking out of his curly hair were two little horns. He carried a flute and was said to live in the wild, where he played music and danced. Because of his connection to nature, he was called the god of the wild, shepherds, and flocks. He was also the god of wooded glens and fields, and the protector of nature. Believers preferred to worship Pan in natural settings, such as caves and grottos.

Pan was a satyr. Satyrs are found in many Greek myths. They are most often men, but later stories featured females, called satyresses. Violet, the switchboard operator, is such a creature. All satyrs are half goat and half human. Not all played flutes, and not all sang and danced. What they did have in common was a fondness for living in the woods and the mountains.

STORY IDEAS

Imagine that you are a satyr. It is a peaceful morning in the meadow. You've been nibbling on the spring grass, listening to the singing of the meadowlark. Then, all of a sudden, one of your flock calls from the distance. "Run to safety! The wolves have left the forest!" What happens next?

★ ★ ★ ★ ★

You and your best friend are taking a walk in the woods. It's a trail you've never been on before. It winds down to a small pond. There, at the edge of the pond, lies a basket. You pull back the cover and find, to your utter amazement, a baby satyr tucked inside. What do you do?

ART IDEA

A satyr is half human and half goat. Now it's time for you to create your own creature that is half human and half whatever you'd like. Maybe you'll choose a well-known animal, like a cat, dog, pig, or elephant. But maybe you'll choose something unusual, like a spider, moth, whale, or peacock. Have fun!

SCIENCE CONNECTION
★ *How to Make Rain* ★

This is an easy experiment you can do in your kitchen. Here's what you need:

A plastic 2-liter soda bottle with a cap
A pair of scissors
Some ice cubes
Some hot water

Make sure that the cap is still on the bottle. Using the scissors, cut the top off the bottle and set it aside. Now fill the bottom of the bottle with one cup hot tap water. Then pick up the bottle top, turn it upside down so that it acts like a cup, and fill it with ice cubes. Then rest the ice-filled top above the hot water.

The sides of the bottle will begin to fog up. Soon, droplets will form and drip off the end of the bottle cap. Why does that happen?

Water can be in three forms—liquid (the stuff we drink), vapor (the invisible water in the air around us), and solid (the ice that cools our sodas).

As warm air rises from the surface of the hot water in the bottle, it carries water molecules. That means some of the liquid water in the bottle has turned into water vapor. As the warm air rises and comes closer to the ice cubes, the air begins to cool. Cool air can't hold as much water vapor as warm air. Why? Because when air turns cold, the air molecules cling closer together and don't leave the water molecules with much room. So the water molecules have only one place to go—down, down, down. And that is why you see water dripping inside your bottle.

This happens in nature as water vapor rises from the warmer earth toward the cooler sky. As the vapor cools, the water is changed back into liquid. This process is called condensation.

So congratulations. By turning liquid water into vapor, then turning that vapor back into liquid water, you've made rain.

CREATIVITY CONNECTION
★ *Yin and Yang* ★

The ancient Chinese symbol of opposites, called a yin-yang symbol, is pretty easy to draw. Here are the instructions:

1. Draw a large circle.

2. Draw a curved line down the middle, almost like a backward *S*, separating the circle into two shapes.

3. Draw two small circles within the larger circle—one at the top and one at the bottom.

4. On one side, color in the small circle, but do not color in the larger shape.

5. On the other side, color in the larger shape, but do not color in the small circle.

6. You've drawn a yin-yang symbol!

ACKNOWLEDGMENTS

Special thanks go to Lynn Brunelle, Emmy Award–winning science writer and science geek extraordinaire, for helping me with the rain experiment. To Gary Pazoff for his help with Grandpa Abe's occasional Yiddish.

And Pam Garfinkel, my new editor. We were a bit scared to be on our own for the first time, but we did it!

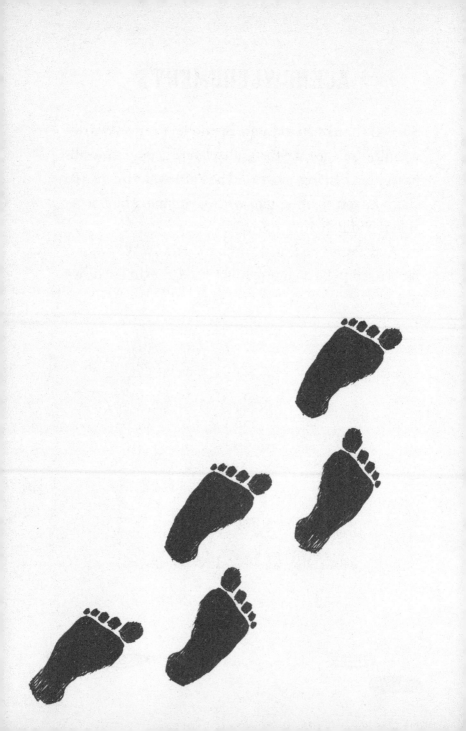

DON'T MISS THE NEXT ADVENTURE

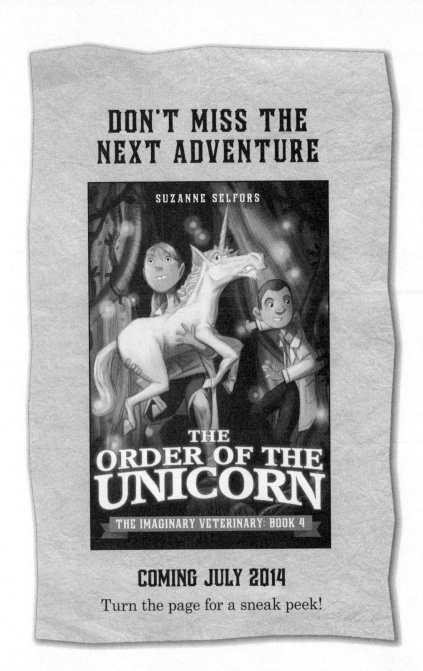

SUZANNE SELFORS

THE ORDER OF THE UNICORN

THE IMAGINARY VETERINARY: BOOK 4

COMING JULY 2014

Turn the page for a sneak peek!

1

PANCAKE SANDWICHES

The first thing many people do after getting out of bed is put on a pair of slippers.

The first thing Pearl Petal did on that Friday morning was slip her feet into a pair of leprechaun shoes.

Shoes made by a real, living, breathing leprechaun.

They fit perfectly around her medium-sized feet. Pink was not her favorite color, but she wasn't about to complain. She'd been told by the leprechaun that the shoes did something special. But he hadn't told her *what*. This lack of information was keeping Pearl awake at night, and she found herself doing very strange things in an attempt to solve the mystery.

The shoes didn't make her fly—that's for sure. She'd tried wearing them while jumping off the kitchen counter and flapping her arms. She'd ended up with a twisted ankle and a scolding from her father. They didn't make her invisible. She'd tried sneaking into the kitchen for a late-night helping of ice cream. Her mother had looked right at her and said, "It's too late for sugar, young lady." They certainly didn't make Pearl strong. She'd tried lifting the car, but all she'd gotten were some weird looks from passersby.

Maybe Cobblestone the leprechaun was a big, fat liar. Or, in this case, a *little*, fat liar. Maybe the shoes did nothing at all.

Even if that proved to be true, no one else in Buttonville had shoes created by a cobbler from the Imaginary World. That fact in itself made Pearl smile.

After opening her bedroom window, Pearl stuck her head outside to see what the morning might bring. Across the street, a flock of pigeons preened their feathers as they perched on the Town Hall roof. The scent of sizzling bacon drifted up from the Buttonville Diner, and Mr. Wanamaker's keys jingled as he opened his barbershop. The morning sky was cloudless, which made Pearl happy. It was also dragonless, which made Pearl extra happy. No clouds meant sunshine. No dragons meant that certain secrets were still... *secret*.

She closed the window. Then her gaze swept across her bedroom shelves, which she'd filled with some of her prized possessions. Her bird-nest collection included nests from a blue jay, a robin, and a hummingbird. But the pigeon's was the most beautiful because pigeons liked to decorate with ribbons, bits of plastic, and buttons.

Pearl's board game collection included Monopoly, Scrabble, and Pony Parade. The goal in Pony Parade was to move a plastic pony from the forest, where it was lost, to its home in the barn. Standing in the way were obstacles, such as a slippery banana peel, a pollywog pond, and a swarm of bees. If you landed on the golden square, you got to trade in your pony for a plastic unicorn. That was Pearl's favorite part. Although she'd outgrown the game, she still longed for a pony. She'd spent a great deal of time trying to persuade her parents to buy one. She'd imagined braiding its mane and riding it around town. "We can keep it in the alley," she'd said when her parents pointed out that they didn't own a barn. Mr. and Mrs. Petal hadn't liked that idea.

Pearl knelt on the carpet and opened the Pony Parade box. She'd hidden three very special pieces of paper inside: a certificate of merit in Sasquatch Catching, a certificate of merit in Curing Lake Monster Loneliness, and a certificate of merit in Rescuing a Rain Dragon. Each certificate was signed by Dr. Emerald Woo, a veterinarian for Imaginary creatures. Now that she'd been working as Dr. Woo's apprentice, something as ordinary as a pony sounded boring. There were so many Imaginary creatures that could be kept in the alley!

"Pearl, Ben's here," her mom, Susan Petal, called from the kitchen.

"Okay. Coming!" As fast as she could, Pearl stuffed the certificates back in the box, then set the game on the shelf. She scrambled out of her pajamas and into her favorite clothes—a plain, well-worn T-shirt and a pair of shiny red basketball shorts. Then she pulled her blond hair into a ponytail and hurried to the kitchen.

"Hi, Ben."

"Hi, Pearl."

Ben Silverstein was sitting at the table. Pearl had only known him for a week, but he'd become her very best friend in the whole world. After all, when two people travel together through interdimensional space, climb the face of a rain dragon, and seal up a hole in her head—not to mention stalk a sasquatch, save a dragon hatchling, and ride in a lake monster's mouth—they can't help but become best friends.

"So nice that you stopped by," Mrs. Petal told Ben. She was standing at the kitchen sink, rinsing the coffeepot. "How's your grandfather?"

"He's fine," Ben said, setting a napkin on his lap. "He's doing some stuff at the senior center this morning."

"Your grandfather's a very nice man." Mrs. Petal was already wearing her work apron, with its embroidered slogan: **YOU GET MORE AT THE DOLLAR STORE**. She dried her hands on a dishtowel. "You kids eat as many pancakes as you like. I'll be unpacking a shipment from China." Then she walked down the stairs and disappeared into the store, which the Petal family owned and operated.

Pearl sat down and grabbed two pancakes. She covered one with syrup, laid four strips of bacon across it, then set another pancake on top. Ben watched with wonder as she picked up her creation with both hands. "What?" she asked. "You've never made a pancake sandwich? It's delicious."

He looked around, as if making sure no one would scold him for bad manners. Then, with a shrug, Ben set aside his fork and grabbed two pancakes. His sandwich had jam in the middle.

"So, what kind of creatures do you think we'll meet today?" Pearl asked. This had become one of her favorite questions.

"Naw deeah," Ben said, which was really "no idea," but his mouth was stuffed.

"I hope we meet a fairy. I really, *really*, REALLY want to meet one." Pearl dipped her sandwich in more syrup. "What size do you think they are? Are they small like a housefly, or maybe big like a bat? Do you think they're pretty? Do you think they can speak our language? Do you—"

Her stream of questions came to a stop. She'd spied something on the table.

Something that made her blood boil.